Black Blood

Lorrie Werden

Black Blood
Copyright © 2018 by Lorrie Werden

All rights reserved. No part of this publication may be reproduced, distributed, or transmitted in any form or by any means, including photocopying, recording, or other electronic or mechanical methods, without the prior written permission of the author, except in the case of brief quotations embodied in critical reviews and certain other non-commercial uses permitted by copyright law.

Tellwell Talent
www.tellwell.ca

ISBN
978-0-2288-0275-4 (Hardcover)
978-0-2288-0276-1 (Paperback)
978-0-2288-0274-7 (eBook)

Acknowledgements

I sincerely wish to acknowledge my dear friend, Sandy Ross, of Word's Worth Communication. She is a wordsmith extraordinaire!

I wish to acknowledge my sincere gratitude to everyone at Tellwell Publishing. Thank you.

I also acknowledge that, although Elizabeth is a fictional character, this book is somewhat autobiographical.

I acknowledge my own struggles with mental illness.

I acknowledge that I have been enveloped by the same darkness as experienced by Elizabeth and have had to find my way back up through that darkness.

I gratefully acknowledge the myriad of doctors, counsellors, friends, family members, and strangers who have helped me gain mental wellness, specifically my Paully, and my Barbie.

Please, if you are struggling with any kind of mental UNwellness, reach out to someone.

In Canada: Crisis Services Canada
1-833-456-4566, or text 45645
In USA: National Suicide Prevention Lifeline
1-800-273-TALK (8255)\

Or visit the following website:
defyingmentalillness.com/worldwide-suicide-helplines
to determine a helpline in your area.

Remember: You are important and your life matters! There are people who care about you! **Please reach out.**

Tabel of Conents

Chapter 1: Acknowledgements i

Chapter 2: Prologue. i

Chapter 3: Halfway There 1

Chapter 4: It Begins. 21

Chapter 5: Panic. 27

Chapter 6: Cursed 35

Chapter 7: Doctor Almighty 43

Chapter 8: Gone. 55

Chapter 9: Confessions 63

Chapter 10: Never the Same. 71

Chapter 11: Two Week Plan 77

Chapter 12: Inner Attack 93

Chapter 13: At the End of Wellington Street 101

Chapter 14: Western Rodeo 113

Chapter 15: A Matter of Self-Control 123

Chapter 16: Never Nana 135

Chapter 17: Inspiration Cometh 143

Chapter 18: And Goeth 149

Chapter 19: Black Blood 185

Chapter 20: Epilogue. 193

Chapter 21: Book Club Discussion Topics. 199

Prologue

The older man sat on the futon, shirtless, his head resting on the back of the thread-bare cushion. His jeans were unzipped and his left hand was tucked inside, fingers wrapped around his scrotum. His legs were spread out before him and were to the right side of the table, one foot resting on a pile of newspapers and magazines. On the table, a small corner had been cleared to hold the little mirror still speckled with bits of cocaine residue that had not been snuffed up into his nostrils. Beside him, a world-worn woman lay curled up, her buttocks pushed up against the man, and her hands covering her ears.

"Honest to God, Maggs. What's the point of the buzz if that fucking kid of yours just keeps screaming?" His voice rose in volume as he spoke the words, trying to be louder than the crying coming from the crib in the next room.

His own daughter, Julia, only five years younger than Margaret, was in the galley kitchenette furiously shaking the baby bottle of dry formula and water. She had not been a participant of this morning's blow fest (nor had she ever) and had turned her back in disgust at the sight that she had come upon 10 minutes earlier. She walked back through the small living room carrying the bottle of formula and, ignoring the situation on the futon, entered the bedroom. She looked at the baby, Elizabeth, squirming in the crib: one sock off, a diaper bulging with urine, and a spit-up encrusted onesie that had lost its snaps long ago. She handed the bottle to the baby who grabbed at it eagerly and popped it into her mouth. Elizabeth was having difficulty in sucking it back while trying to inhale through her snot covered nose, so Julia used the edge of a receiving blanket to wipe away the offending mucous. Elizabeth breathed easier then, and was able to gulp down the rest of the bottle.

Julia grabbed a fresh Huggies from the bag, found a clean sleeper, and tucked them under her arm. Sated, Elizabeth stood up in her crib, threw the now empty bottle over the side, laughed at her clever trick, then laughed again as a large belch escaped her. Julia picked her up out of the crib and set her little, unsteady legs on the floor. She tucked her own index fingers into Elizabeth's little clenched fists and stretched the pudgy arms upward. "OK, Little Bit. Let's go." Together, they baby-stepped toward the bathroom.

Once inside the room, Elizabeth instinctively released Julia's fingers and placed her chubby hands on the edge of the tub. Her little legs pumped up and down in excitement as warm water splashed into the awaiting vessel. Julia whipped off the saturated diaper and plunked it in the full and overflowing basket. Gotta empty that today, Julia thought. She pulled off the undershirt and, after checking the temperature once again to ensure it was not too hot, lifted Elizabeth into the little pool of water. Elizabeth squealed with delight. She stretched out her legs and her toes splayed and wiggled happily. Those chubby little hands found the water and splashed until the soft blond down of her head was drenched, and her long eyelashes were darkened and exaggerated from the cascading water.

Busy puffing on a cigarette as she sat on the toilet seat, Julia let her play. Elizabeth rolled over onto her tummy and blew bubbles on the water. She kicked her feet, sending water onto Julia who laughingly scolded the baby. "Oh! Little Bit! You got Jules all wet." This made Elizabeth laugh harder and she kicked again with delight. Her smoke finished, Julia reached into the tub and turned the toddler over onto her back. She offered her a soft plastic teething ring to occupy her hands while Julia washed her hair with a squirt of Johnson's. Elizabeth played happily and did not fuss even when the water accidentally ran over her eyes. She merely shook her head, blinked her eyes, and continued to splash her now wrinkled toes. Lifting Elizabeth into a sitting position, and using the few bubbles of remaining shampoo, Julia ran her hand gently along Elizabeth's back, under her arms, and under the folds of her double chin. A washcloth came next to fluff up the few yellow curls and to wipe away any remnants of soap from Elizabeth's skin.

Julia pulled a deeply creased towel from off the floor and brought it to her nose to smell. Still usable. Returning to sit on the toilet seat, she draped the towel over her knees, then bent forward to lift the little girl onto her lap. While she chewed on the teething ring, Elizabeth allowed Julia to dry her with the prickly, brittle towel. Julia lifted Elizabeth and pulled the towel from her lap to spread it out flat onto the floor. Once Elizabeth was lying on the towelled floor, a diaper was applied to the exposed bottom and Elizabeth was dressed in the pink sleepers with images of shiny Gummi Bears emblazoned on her chest.

Julia and Elizabeth returned to the living room area and, upon passing the futon, Elizabeth began to babble. "Mumm, mummm. Mummy. Mummm, mumm, mumm." She arched her back way from Julia and, twisting her body, outstretched her arms toward the curled figure on the couch.

Without rousing herself from her place of rest, a sluggish voice squeaked, "Hey, mama's baby. You gonna get some nummies?" Julia plunked the warm bundle into the high chair and took two steps into the kitchenette. She pulled a Rusk from the nearly empty bag on the counter and presented it to Elizabeth who grabbed it and chewed on it hungrily. Julia opened the cupboard doors and looked at the selection of junior baby food jars: squash, peas and carrots, a chicken stew concoction, and two jars of peaches. She reached for the fruit and informed the living room, "You're gonna hafta get this kid some food soon. She's got, like, enough food for today, but then she's out."

The female figure in the living room wiped at her face attempting to push the hair out of her eyes. She stretched awkwardly as she tried to avoid kicking the man, knocking over the table, or hitting her arms on the wall behind her head. She sat up and, realizing that stringy hair was still blocking her vision, she tried again to move it out of her eyes. She blinked furiously in an attempt to focus, or awaken from her haze, or to just see into the heavily curtained, dark room. "What's the date?" she asked the kitchen.

"It's the twenty-first," came the reply.

There was a stirring of excitement from the woman on the futon. She pushed on the leg of the man beside her who was still riding his buzz. "Come on," she exclaimed. "The baby bonus will be here today! We gotta get some shit for the kid, and I'll call Rog to get some more stuff for us." She reached a boy finger toward the mirror, wiped some residue off the square, and applied it along her gum line. She pushed the man again and repeated sternly, "Come on!" She rose as the man grumbled for her to fuck off, but he, too, rose and followed her.

Julia stood in front of Elizabeth, put a less than clean bib around her neck and fed her the peaches from out of the jar. Elizabeth slurped and swallowed the fruit between bites of the cracker. She babbled and cooed during the entire feeding, happily talking to Julia, calling out to her mother, and experimented making raspberry noises, squeals, and tongue clicks.

Margaret emerged from the bedroom. Her hair was pulled back from her face and held in place by a plastic headband. She had pulled on balloon pants and a t-shirt, both of which hung from her skeletal figure. "Do you have a smoke I can bum?" she asked Julia. Julia pulled a cigarette from the package tucked in her back pocket and tossed it to Margaret. "Thanks," she said as she returned to her seat on the futon. "I'll buy you a pack today when we're out." She paused to flick on the lighter, inhaled, and, blowing out the smoke added, "You gonna be OK with the baby?"

Julia spooned the last of the peaches into the little opened mouth in front of her. "Maggs," she said, controlling her rising anger. "Today is Tuesday. I gotta go to school. I've got my chem exam this morning and biology this afternoon." She could hear Margaret's audible sigh. Julia wiped Elizabeth's chin with the bib and tried to get the gluey Rusk cracker off the fingers. She asked Margaret, "Did you take your pills?"

Again, another audible sigh reached Julia, but this time it was followed by a "Christ Almighty. You'd think you were my goddamned keeper." Margaret rose and walked past Julia into the kitchen. From the corner of her eye, Julia watched as Margaret opened three bottles, extracted a pill from each one, replaced the lids, and gathered the pills into her hand. She turned on the water at the sink and bent over so she could suck water from the faucet. She tossed back the pills, then tossed the three bottles back into the cupboard.

Julia picked Elizabeth up from the high chair and put her in the playpen. When the coke was out, Elizabeth needed to be sequestered somewhere in safety. Besides, it was the only clear space in which Elizabeth could practise walking. The rest of the floored areas were covered with strewn clothing, the stroller, a grocery cart, books, and boxes of her dad's clothes. Thankfully, when they were able to get this apartment, the second little bedroom had been given to Julia so that she did not have to live in the upheaval of the living room. Once she was done secondary school, she thought happily, she was out of here anyway. She had received confirmation of her place at Humber College and had been approved for OSAP. Just two more months and she was on her way.

"Dad," Julia yelled through the closed bathroom door, "Don't forget to take your pills." Julia picked up her backpack from the floor and grabbed her textbooks from off the small table that served as her desk. She flung the pack over her shoulder and looked at Margaret who was reclining on the futon, head back, eyes closed. "Maggs, I gotta go. You OK to watch Little Bit now?"

Margaret sat up from the cushion and glared at Julia. "Her fucking name is Elizabeth and of course I am OK to watch her." She used air quotes when she said OK. She rose from the couch and walked toward the baby. Two little arms went up and Margaret scooped to pick up the bundle. "Of course mama is OK to watch my precious baby." With Elizabeth resting on her hip, Margaret swayed her body back and forth and her voice became sing-songie. "We'll go to the bank and get some money. We'll get some food for my honey. Then we'll get some sugar for your mommy." Margaret laughed at her own rhyming ingenuity.

Julia moved to the coffee table, lifted up the shiny drug server, and carried it to the kitchen where she placed it on the small counter top. She walked past the cooing mother and child and popped a quick kiss on Elizabeth's head before exiting. Poor little pumpkin, she thought as she closed the door behind her. You don't stand a chance.

As she reached the sidewalk, she looked back up at the apartment window and fervently hoped that they'd be all right until she returned.

– 1 –

Halfway There

Elizabeth stood at the sink, waiting for Matron, and watched as her hands performed the horrifically disgusting task of washing the breakfast dishes. She hated having her hands in the water, especially when she didn't need to be cleansed, but she had requested that washing the dishes become her new job, her new responsibility, so she could show them that she was working very hard "towards re-entering society as a productive and valuable citizen." Bullshit. She just wanted to be the hell out of this halfway house. She and the other nine socially misfit women with whom she shared the complex—they all just wanted out. They merely faked and counterfeited their way through the required classes and counselling sessions that were (supposed to be) the definitive starting point in their newly legal, or medically mandated 'healing' process. They attended their classes, stuck to their prescribed schedules, and took advantage of the minimal freedoms given to them, just waiting for the day when they'd stand in judgement before Doctor Almighty who had the power to rubber stamp their files with the glorious word, 'REHABILITATED.' Once that was done, they could return to the streets where they would score again, slut again, die again. Everyone was the same. They just wanted out.

Elizabeth was the only member of the house who didn't have a criminal record. She wasn't an ex-con, or a junkie, or a whore, but the rules and routines placed upon her by Doctor Almighty, and enforced by the rotating shifts of Rotund Ugly Matrons, were just as strict as they were for the newly paroled, needle-pushing paramours. Up before 7:00, showered and dressed, and down to the common kitchen area by 7:30. There, they'd trip over one another trying to feed their bodies, stuff their souls, and gratify their aching with something, anything, that might replace the hunger for their particular addiction of choice.

After breakfast, they'd each clamour towards the sink, banging religiously into the protruding island that stood as a barrier between the kitchen and the eating area, shower it with blasphemed curses, then continue forward to be the first to clean her dishes. This task was done, not really as an attempt at improving her housekeeping skills as was the intention, but so she could then race to be the first one to stand before whichever Rotund Ugly Matron was her saviour for the day. Here, each woman would receive her communion, her first round of medication needed to fight off the earthly demons.

Black Blood

While nine other women received a withdrawal Eucharist (or some other kind of shit), Elizabeth took a specialty drug cocktail designed just for her by Doctor Almighty. With all his power and wizardry he had concocted a brew of medications with lithium this, sodium that, and even some 'pines and 'zines thrown into the mixture to help tame the bipolar disorder that plagued her.

After receiving the drug sacrament—*Bless me, Matron, for I have sinned; it's been three weeks since my last illegal injection*—each woman would continue on with the guise of leading a normal life. Some went to literacy classes. Some went to part-time jobs at Walmart or Goodwill—jobs that their social workers had helped them to procure. Some went to parenting classes. Elizabeth scoffed at this. Parenting classes! Really? Did they honestly think that by staying clean for a month or two and by taking some stupid classes that they would have a remote hope in hell of being able to parent their children again? Nope.

And some, like Elizabeth, went to counselling sessions.

After her first dosing of the day, Elizabeth's daily regime continued after breakfast when she retreated to her bedroom to record the morning's thoughts and feelings in the little blue book that Dr. Anderson (oh, yes, Doctor Almighty had a real name, a bland name plastered all over his office wall) had given to her as part of her therapy. Last month, when she was admitted to the hospital during a nasty paranoid cycle, her thoughts were solely focused on the black cells. They had coursed through her body and she rapidly lost the battle to cleanse herself of them. She'd been off her meds for several weeks by then and, just as Dr. Anderson had warned her, going off the medication triggered the black cells to come back. And they had.

On the evening that the black cells rapidly replaced the red blood cells, she became frenzied in trying to rid herself of them. At first, there were only a few in her thumb. She could see them through her skin and she snapped her attention to them to see if they were spreading or if they had just settled there. The spreading cells scared her the most. They multiplied quickly and, just as if lead had been injected into the cells, they would become heavy and stagnant in their place. This immobility of the cells would cause two problems. First, with the heaviness of the blackness, she was unable to move in whatever part of her body the cells were. Secondly, when the black cells replaced the red ones, there were fewer good cells to carry oxygen and nutrients to the rest of her body. She knew that, without the life-saving red blood cells, she would die.

On that particular night, the black cells multiplied quickly. She tried to rub them out of her thumb, but that only spread them into her palm. In the bathroom sink, she washed and scrubbed her hand in an effort to dissolve them, but that didn't work. She ran from her bathroom, tripped down the stairs and ran to the kitchen looking for something that would help in cleaning them away. She grabbed a sponge from the cupboard under the kitchen sink but realized that she didn't have anything coarse enough to help eradicate the cells. Anxiously scanning the cupboards and the counter, it suddenly occurred to her that the only thing that could help her now was something botanical like sea water, or algae, or sand. But where, oh, where, could she find that? Her mind flashed through a thousand pictures of seas and oceans, lakes and streams, ponds and puddles. Then it struck her. The fountain in Victoria Park. She knew there was green algae sticking to the sides of the bowl of the fountain. She just knew that the algae would leech into her skin and disrupt the pH balance enough that it would destroy the black cells and allow new red cells to be created.

She knew she had to act quickly before the black cells began to prevent movement in her arm. She carried the sponge with her as she fled her apartment and gained access to the elevator. She held her left arm close to her body as she hopped from one bare foot to the other waiting for the elevator. Once the doors pinged open, she thrust herself into the box and pushed 'G.' It seemed to take an eternity for the elevator to traverse the three storeys to ground level and Elizabeth continued to bounce anxiously. Once the elevator reached its destination, Elizabeth broke out, ran through the lobby, and struck the barred door with her right hand so that it would open. She jumped down the three concrete steps and from there, she turned right to run along the middle of Pall Mall Street until she came to Wellington. She cut sharply across the road and ran blindly through the night toward her goal.

Lorrie Werden

The harder she ran, though, the more the black cells came. They were already immobilizing her shoulder and, if she didn't hurry, they would start to strangle her if they rose upward into her throat. She couldn't let them take over her vocal cords so she began to scream in the hope that by using the muscles needed for speech and for breathing, the black cells would find a different route to go. She knew her breathing was laboured from running and she started to feel nauseous. She could just make out the lights along the corner of Victoria Park, calling her forward. She pushed on through the dark, passing parked cars along the side of the road and the young men who were milling about on the street. Somebody called out to her, but she couldn't respond. She just continued to run and scream.

She reached the grass of Victoria Park and made her way to the fountain. In the dark, it was hard to see the algae, and the grounded lights that shone upwards toward the fountain glared in her eyes and made it nearly impossible for Elizabeth to see anything. She knelt down beside the fountain, thrust her arms into the water and began scraping the sides of the fountain with the sponge, hoping that there was algae there to transfer onto her skin. She knew she had stopped screaming, but she was still crying and muttering. Please! Let there be algae. I have to scrub them away. I have to scrub!

She was urgently rubbing the sponge along her left arm when she heard a voice behind her and then felt a hand land on her shoulder. A hand on her shoulder! Her left shoulder—the shoulder immobilized by the black cells. Incensed, she screamed for the hand to be removed. Didn't they know that their touch could kill her? Were they trying to kill her? Was the outstretched hand meant to rapidly increase her death? Elizabeth wrenched herself away from the hand and climbed into the basin of the fountain to distance herself from the stranger. She placed her back against the middle of the fountain in an effort to barricade herself from the few people who had gathered there. She sunk down and allowed the water to spread over herself and, from the safety of the fountain, she barked at the people to leave her alone and begged them not to touch her. She continued to scrub her arm and, with the water now surrounding her, she was able to scrub her neck and her chest. The cells were spreading across her chest and she moved the sponge like an eraser, back and forth, to try to erase them. From the scrubbing though, her t-shirt had become entangled in the sponge and prevented the sponge from actually touching her chest. Frustrated that the shirt was interfering with her cleansing, she pulled it off, allowing her breasts to be exposed so that she could cleanse them, too.

While she scrubbed, the black cells began to dissipate. She had been sobbing uncontrollably as fear had shaken her to her very core, but now, with the cells receding, her frantic crying became simple moans, extended sighs of relief, and snuffling of her nose. The cells were gone now from her chest, and her shoulder felt unhindered. As she looked at her thumb, she noted that the black cells had even gone from there.

She sat back in the water, inhaled haltingly, and realized that somebody was talking to her.

"Ma'am? Can you hear me? My name is Nathan and I'm a paramedic. I'm here to help you." Elizabeth ran her hand over her eyes and tried to focus on the face emitting the voice. With her eyes returning to normal, she could see the flashing lights of the ambulance and wondered when they had gotten there?

"I had to wash the black cells," she said to the voice. "They were killing me."

"I understand that, Ma'am. Are you able to step out of the fountain now? May I help you?"

Elizabeth slowly stood and offered her hand to the man. She stepped out of the fountain and a blanket was immediately thrown over her shoulders. A gurney was there and she allowed Nathan to help her sit down on it. Nathan spoke with her while he took her vitals and explained what he was doing when he hooked her up to an IV. Elizabeth could hear his voice in radio contact with the hospital, but she couldn't make out exactly what he was saying. She did understand, though, when he told her that he thought it would be best if she was seen by a doctor, so, with her consent, she was lifted up into the ambulance and taken to the hospital.

Once she got to the hospital, everything happened very quickly. Doctor Almighty was called and, under his command, she was admitted. He prescribed medication for her, but Elizabeth had slipped into immobility. The nurses came and got her up, bathed her, and clothed her. She would sit in a chair until they moved her. Aides tried to feed her, but Elizabeth's mouth could not chew. Straw-laden, thickened drinks were offered to her and she instinctively swallowed the concoction, but had no sensation of doing so. Deep within her soul she knew they were getting medications into her, but she wasn't sure how. Probably in the liquids or maybe through the IV. She couldn't even tell if she was still hooked up or not and it really didn't matter to her.

By day three, she was coming around. The drugs were drawing her out of the catatonic state into which she had escaped. She'd continued to grow more alert and was functioning better and, by the end of the second week in hospital, she was well enough to leave her chartreuse coloured room and take up guarded residence at the halfway house.

Oh, but taking the meds! God how she hated them! Although they had brought her out of the depths of the catatonic state, they stifled her somewhere between reality and 'zombification.' When she was fully in the stabilizing clutches of the medications, her beautiful, creative mind would solidify under the weight of their control and she couldn't paint. The visions and images that transcended from her spiritual communication with the universe would suddenly stop. There were no divine messages of what to paint, where to paint it, or how to paint it. There was no inspiration. She felt only the weight of the freezing, an induced fog, as if Novocaine had been syringed directly into her cerebral cortex.

Lorrie Werden

When she was shipped to the halfway house for observation and treatment, she continued to receive her daily prescribed drug communion from the various Rotund Ugly Matrons, as well as behavioural therapy counselling from Doctor Almighty. In the time since she had arrived, she had progressed so well that they had even allowed her to retrieve her paints (under the watchful eye of Matron Ronnie) from her apartment.

With her brain not yet completely frozen from the medication, it was still able to create and she had painted a truly inspired, masterful, wonderful picture of Heaven and Hell. The vibrant blues and purples swirled and dipped on the canvas to create the dancing of angel's wings, while God's gentle voice was displayed as streaks of cadmium yellow as it descended to man. As the viewer's eyes travelled across the painting, the enlightening power of the canvas changed. Various shades of black combined with flames of blood red, and leapt up from the bottom of the canvas drawing the viewer from the soft comfort of God's angels into the damning pits of hell. The dark and reflective shapes drew you closer to the picture, compelling you to search the black and grey shadows for your own soul, holding you there as you held your breath until unconsciousness begged, staring, searching for your reflection; positive that it would be there, but praying that it wasn't. Then, when your lungs were about to burst and you won the battle to breathe, you could shift yourself away from the picture. Once released from its power though, your body reacted with a shuddering repulsion of the evil that had spread through you while you had been transfixed in its presence. Elizabeth knew Yvonne would want it for her gallery. It was a masterpiece.

This week, her inspiration was not as powerful. She'd painted, but had not felt inspired. Her roomies said her latest landscape was good, really good. They loved the wispy bits of white that represented sheep (why the hell was she painting sheep?), the stout, brown, curved lines of branches topped with green tapped flecks that arched over the speckled wheat field, and the secret shadow of an outbuilding surrounded by the lazy, cobalt fence. Elizabeth, however, was totally dissatisfied with it. She hated it. She had felt no divine inspiration for this painting and she felt that the picture had merely plunked from her hand onto the canvas. She knew the effects of the medication were already starting to numb her brain, and she had to get off them so she could better receive true inspiration. That was going to be difficult, as she had three more weeks of this mandatory treatment before she could return to her apartment and lead her own life, her own reality.

The idea of being in charge of washing the morning dishes developed during the week when the Martha-Stewart-wannabe arrived at the house. Martha, in all her 300 pounds of glory, had just been transferred from Six E, the outpatient psych ward at St. Benedict's Hospital on Richmond Street, after an 'incident' with a male nurse. Until the hospital's lawyers could prove who seduced whom, Martha was here until other arrangements could be made for Mr. Nurse.

Lorrie Werden

On her first day there, Martha wasn't scheduled to see Doctor Almighty until 10:30 so she continued to sit while the other women bumped by her in their efforts to reach the sink. This was no easy task for the women, as the larger-than-life Martha was uncomfortably, and unfortunately, seated at the island that separated the cabinetry from the eating area. After the fourth woman struck her with an elbow as she passed to go around the island to get to the sink, the old broad jumped up and shrieked, "Jesus Christ! Just give me the goddamned dishes and get the fuck out of here!" She pushed her way past the other women and began filling the sink with hot water. From her vantage point at the dining table, Elizabeth stared at her in incredulity as she watched Martha turn to the island, unlock its tiny silver brakes, and pull it close to her, creating a barrier between herself and the women. Martha was completely surrounded by the U-shaped cupboards and the island, and the only way to reach her was to stand on the opposite side of the island across from her. As the women neared her, they created a nice, orderly line-up in front of the island, then cautiously held out their dishes which Martha Stewart then plucked from their hands and deposited into the sink. When the last woman had backed away, Martha went about the business of cleaning the kitchen. She methodically washed the dishes, wiped off the table where Elizabeth was seated (she quietly resigned her empty coffee cup to Martha), wiped the counter and the stove, repositioned the island, dabbed the crumbs away from the toaster, rinsed Elizabeth's mug, swept the floor, returned jams and spreads to the refrigerator, and set the air dried dishes in their proper cupboards.

Elizabeth was privy to Martha Stewart's masterful domination for only four days, but as she sat and watched this exhibition, she noticed something very interesting that happened in the kitchen each of those mornings. Martha Stewart took such a long time to clean the kitchen that the Matron, who needed to continue with her own chores of the day, carried into the kitchen the little paper cup containing Martha's drug mélange. There, at precisely 8:45 a.m., standing on the opposite side of the island, Matron deposited the pills into Martha's left hand. Matron then watched her take a drink, checked to ensure the pills had been swallowed, and left her to continue with her dishwashing tasks.

After watching this routine for the fourth day in a row, Elizabeth had an idea. With Martha being returned to the hospital tomorrow, Elizabeth requested to speak with the head Matron. "I notice," she said to Matron Bernice once she had been granted an interview, "that the kitchen is much calmer in the morning when the ensconced women are able to hand over their dishes to our latest visitor." She didn't use the visitor's name—she didn't even know it. "I am aware that my fellow companions have scheduled events for which they must not be late: classes, work, counselling. I, on the other hand, have nary to do until I meet with Dr. Anderson at 10:00. I wondered," she continued as she placed her hand on her heart to indicate the seriousness of her offer, "if I could, therefore, have the humbling responsibility of doing the dishes and cleaning up the kitchen for my fellow detainees? I could use this time to interact with each woman and then record which social skills I was able to use with them. I would have just enough time to impart these lessons into my book of records before seeing Dr. Anderson." Looking directly at Matron Bernice she said, "I would greatly appreciate the opportunity of being able to provide this service to the legion of my fellow women so that I can be of valuable service to them." She lowered her gaze and bowed her head, as she awaited the verbal anointment from the Matron.

"Well," said Matron Bernice. There was a pause, and when Elizabeth raised her head, she saw a smiling, sunny Matron returning her gaze. Elizabeth recognized the smile and was actually quite impressed that she had been able to extract it from Matron. It was the smile Matron reserved for Dr. Anderson when she spoke about the women who were successfully completing their therapy programs. It was almost the smile she gave to the rehabilitated women as she sent them, with God's blessing, back into the depths from which they had come, momentarily restored and renewed, but ready to jump back into their former lives that were just around the corner, beckoning them with hypodermic fingers, to return to the streets because they had nowhere else to go.

"I think that is a gracious and wonderful idea," Matron Bernice said. "I will discuss it with Dr. Anderson and I will let you know later this afternoon." When Elizabeth was dismissed, she returned to her room where a plan began carefully percolating in her head.

Black Blood

At 2:00, the Slut from Simcoe tapped on Elizabeth's door to inform her that Matron Bernice wanted to see her. Elizabeth was both nervous and excited to think that not only had she been granted an interview with the Matron so quickly, but that Matron might actually have some good news for her.

"I have spoken with Dr. Anderson," Matron said once Elizabeth was seated in her office, "and he thinks this is a wonderful idea. He is particularly pleased that you initiated this gesture on your own, Elizabeth, and feels it is a sure sign that your medication is stabilizing. You may begin washing the breakfast dishes tomorrow morning, after which time you will see Dr. Anderson to discuss how the procedure went, your thoughts and feelings on assisting your friends, and anything else you and he should like to discuss."

Elizabeth stood up gracefully and slowly. Although her insides were doing a conga line, she had no intention of letting Matron know her exhilaration. "Thank you," she graciously accepted, resisting the urge to bow, "for granting me the running of the torch of dishwashing. I won't disappoint you or Dr. Anderson." She turned and left Matron's office and resisted the urge to pee herself with excitement. The plan to be in control of which medications she would take was rapidly coming together.

Once she started the task the next morning, it took only three days to perfect the move that would allow her to control the doses of medication. First, she ensured that the island was propped closely enough so that she could be reached only if someone stood across from the island. The relocation of the island was nothing new for the other residents; the Martha-Stewart-wannabe had already started that routine and, since Matron had served Martha the medications from across the island, Elizabeth had no doubt this practice would continue for her. Elizabeth's true task was learning how to expel six small items from her mouth without being noticed. At exactly 8:30 for three consecutive mornings, Elizabeth practised the expulsion in front of the few unsuspecting housemates who remained in the kitchen. She got six frozen peas from the freezer, each one representing one of her medications. She placed the peas in her mouth and wrapped both hands around a mug in which there was very little water. She didn't actually need a drink for her plan to work, and she certainly didn't need the water for cleansing the black cells right now either, but the mug was a very important player in her plan. She turned her body so that her left hip was beside the island and she raised the mug to her lips. Then, while holding her hands tight to her face as she gripped the cup, she pretended to drink. The exaggerated motion of moving her lower jaw up and down appeared to be the gulping of the pills into her body, but it was actually the motion of her tongue as it expelled the peas from her mouth into her right hand. This was the hand farthest from the island, hidden by the mug, and thus unseen from Matron's staring eyes. Even better was the fact that this hand was covered in soap bubbles to help hide the peas—a terrible taste for Elizabeth if her tongue got too far past the mug, but one she was able

Black Blood

to ignore if it meant disposing of the pills. Once the six peas had been expelled into her right hand, she flattened it against the mug to hold the peas in place, then lowered her hands and the mug down into the sink, taking the frozen peas deep into the soapy water, buried beneath the bubbles. For those first three days of practice, any woman who was still in the kitchen and lay witness to Elizabeth's opened mouth grin and exposed tongue as proof that her mouth was now empty, did not remain in the kitchen long enough to question her motive. They merely gaped at her awkwardly as they left the room.

On the fourth day, Monday, Elizabeth felt ready to perform the pill switch with Matron. She had finished washing all the dishes, but had not yet drained the sink. Her right hand stroked the wet sponge to create a mass of thick, white foam that covered her fingers, her palm, and the back of her hand, ensuring there were enough bubbles to camouflage the trickery that Elizabeth was about to execute. Her left hand was wet, but free from suds, and her nearly empty mug was poised at the back of the sink ready for its part in her ruse.

At exactly 8:45, Matron Bernice entered the kitchen. She was carrying the little paper chalice of Elizabeth's medication in her thick hands, and she greeted Elizabeth with, "Still at it, eh?" Elizabeth smiled, nodded, and reached for the small paper cup with her left hand. She tipped the pills onto the end of her tongue, gave the paper cup back to Matron, and reached with both hands for the dark mug at the back of the sink. When she raised the mug to her mouth, she had already pushed the pills between her gums and her cheek. She ensured her left hand covered the gap between her mouth and the mug, while her right hand, out of Matron's sight, cupped at the corner of her mouth so she could expel the six malevolent meds into it.

The task was more difficult than she had thought it would be. The previous practice with the peas had allowed her to expel small orbs, but some of these medications were big and oblong. The exaggerated swallowing motion took place as her tongue fumbled to force a few pills into her right hand, but she wasn't able to get them all out. She couldn't push the bigger ones one for fear that she would have to open her mouth too widely, thus allowing pills to perhaps fall onto the floor, and she couldn't risk having her plan blown so soon after its implementation. Knowing that she had now spent too much time pretending to drink, she flattened her hand against the cup, and swallowed the remaining meds with the bit of water from the mug. Holding the unknown meds tightly, she then lowered them, the mug, and the soap, down into the sink, then turned her head toward Matron to allow the oral inspection. Matron smiled, turned, and left Elizabeth alone in the kitchen.

Once Matron was gone, Elizabeth searched the sink to try to determine which pills she had taken. Shit! She didn't know which drugs were for anything; she had always just taken whatever Doctor Almighty had given her. Well, she thought, it was an accomplishment of sorts. She took a long, deep, inhale of breath that she forced out in an audible sigh and pondered her predicament for a few moments. But then she smiled. Now that she had actually felt the pills in her mouth, she would be able, on the next occasion, to fashion her tongue into a better scoop from which to push out the pills. She succumbed to the delight at her deception. She pulled the plug and, as some remaining bubbles reached the drain, Elizabeth opened the faucet to let the water flush away the pills with the bits of leftover egg and toast crumbs down the drain, just another bit of breakfast crap to be washed away.

– 2 –

It Begins

I am six years old. I have lived with my Nana for three years. I did not go to Junior Kindergarten and I missed most of Senior Kindergarten. They sent a lady out from the school board to talk to my Nana, to try to discover why I was absent for so many days. The lady called the Children's Aid Society who hooked us up with Ellen Jackson, Social Worker. Ellen made sure that Nana had transportation every Thursday to and from the grocery store. She made sure that I had a regular bedtime, and that Nana learned how to set the new alarm clock so she could get me up in time for school. The only thing Ellen didn't have any concerns about was my cleanliness. Cleanliness was never an issue with any of the social workers we had (oh, yes, there were many more to come), as Nana spent most of her time cleaning. Every day, all day, she cleaned. She started with the breakfast dishes. She washed them, disinfected them, rinsed them, dried them, and returned them to the cupboard. She wiped down the walls, scoured the floors, and took an old toothbrush to the tiles in the backsplash. She continued her cleaning ritual into the living room, the bedrooms and the bathroom, carrying with her the arsenal of cleaning products.

Then it was lunch time and after we had eaten, she started the kitchen cleaning all over again. Then she did laundry. She washed the sheets and towels and our dirty clothes. Supper came and went; she cleaned the kitchen again then, when she was done that, she washed me. I sat in the tub as she scrubbed my face and my neck. She put her hands on my shoulders and turned me so my back was facing her. She washed all down my back and across my shoulders. She placed her thumb and forefinger around the wrist of my left arm and extended it out to the side so she could scrub from my shoulder to my wrist with the cloth. She did the same with my right arm, but when she was finished washing it, she used her grip on that wrist to spin my body back so it faced the drain again. Then she washed my stomach and my legs. She scrubbed each foot and in between each toe, but then she threw the washcloth at me, turned her back and said, "Wash there." I swished the cloth around my private parts, dragged it around to my back, and made a few swipes at my buttocks. It was my job to pull the plug, stand up in the tub with my back to Nana, and wait until she put the towel around my shoulders. When I went to my bedroom to get into my pajamas, Nana cleaned the tub, wiped the floor where the water had dripped, and dried off the bar of soap before replacing it in the soap dish.

Black Blood

At night, I sat with her while she watched the television, then went to bed when I was tired.

In November of the year I went into Grade One, Nana suddenly rediscovered her religion. She was flipping through the television stations when she came upon a program called, Midday Mass. *The priest was talking and his words came right through that television screen and landed right on Nana. He said that the moral fibre of society was deteriorating and it was our responsibility, as Catholics, to ensure that our children were being raised in the Catholic faith. Nana looked at me, looked back at the television, and clicked her tongue.*

I was immediately transferred from Johnston Elementary School (the school that was just around the corner from our house and where Nana walked me on the days that I went) to St. Theresa's, a thirty-five minute bus ride from our house. Nana was elated. She was doing her part to ensure that THIS child was being raised in the Catholic faith—and she didn't even have to get dressed. She just had to stand, in her pajamas, at the door and push me toward the looming, yellow bus. Then, to her great pleasure, she could return to the house and her cleaning.

On my first day at St. Theresa's, I didn't know anyone, or anything. I followed the other children from the bus into the school and waited by the door until a man came out of an office and squatted down in front of me. "And what might your name be?" he asked.

I lowered my head and whispered, "Elizabeth."

Lorrie Werden

"Ah, the new girl. Let me show you around." He led me down the hall and ushered me into a classroom. He introduced me to the teacher, but then he left. He didn't show me anything else. He didn't show me where the lunch room was or where the playground was. He didn't even show me where the bathroom was and, later that afternoon when we got let out for last recess, I couldn't hold it any longer. I had an accident. I stood in a corner by the fence and cringed as the warmth ran down between my legs and into my shoes. Then I cringed again as the warmth of tears ran down my cheeks. A big kid told the teacher on yard duty that I'd pissed myself. "Jacob! Don't use that language at school." She came toward me. I was embarrassed and I turned my face into the fence to try to avoid her. She didn't speak to me. She got a different big kid to take me back to my class. My teacher found a pair of underwear for me, showed me where the bathroom was, and, once I was changed, she put my pee soaked underwear in a plastic bag. At the end of the day, I rode the bus home, carrying my pee soaked pants. The bigger kids noticed the bag. They had heard about my accident and called me Pisshead.

When I got home, Nana was appalled. I had been potty trained long before I came to live with her and she had never had to deal with soiled clothing. The bag with the wet clothes was wrenched from my hands and thrown immediately into the kitchen trash. That trash bag was then gathered up, sealed, and taken out to the big silver garbage can at the side of the house. When Nana came back in, she grabbed my arm and dragged me up the stairs into the bathroom. She put the plug in the tub and began filling it with hot water. She didn't add any cold. After she ripped off my dress and threw it into a big green garbage bag that had miraculously manifested in her hands, she told me to take off the alien underwear and deposit it, too, into the bag. She tied this bag up and carried it downstairs. I know she put it outside in the big silver garbage can because I heard the back door open, bang shut, then open, and bang shut again. She came back upstairs and went directly to the sink to scrub her hands. Then, she swooped me up and stood me in the tub. The water was boiling hot and I cried out in pain.

"Shut up," she growled as she turned off the water that had risen to my ankles. "You did this. You made this mess. You clean it up." She threw a washcloth into the water, stood back from the tub, and told me to wash.

I continued to cry. Not so much from the pain, but because I was just so totally overwhelmed: overwhelmed by Nana's anger, overwhelmed by my first day at a new school, overwhelmed by the long bus ride, overwhelmed by the big kids who had made fun of me. When I bent down to pick up the washcloth, I could see that my feet were red and bloated. They felt heavy. Solid. Too heavy to move. In my little six year old brain, I needed to understand why they were so big, so swollen, and so sore. The scalding hot water, I reasoned (for I dare not ask Nana why), had made all the blood in my body rush to my feet, making them swell, making them feel solid. They were like cement, heavy, and dark. As I continued to look at them, the most horrifying thing in the world happened. My ankles turned black. Right before my very eyes I watched as the hot water burned all the blood cells in my ankles and feet. The heat from the hot water had singed all my blood cells and turned my feet black. I was shocked. I was scared. I continued to crouch and cry, mesmerized by my black feet. I heard Nana scream at me, "Elizabeth! Pay attention." She grabbed my arm and jerked me into standing.

And that was the first time I saw the black cells.

– 3 –

Panic

On this, the seventh day of doing the horrifically insulting task of washing dishes and, being the fourth day of self-regulated medication, Elizabeth had to remind herself that this was her idea and that she needed to stick to her plan. The problem with doing the dishes was two-fold. First, she hated having her hands in the water. She actually only needed water for the socially required ritual of daily showering, and then for the much more involved ritual of cleansing herself of the black cells when they came. Since she had already taken her daily required shower, she did not need to have her hands in this filthy, dirty water, and she was aggravated that her hands had to be thrust into this slime when they didn't need to be cleansed. She could feel her anxiety rising and knew that the water was the cause of the elevation. She knew too, though, that she had to stick to her plan of doing the dishes so she could continue to regulate her own medications.

Lorrie Werden

Her second problem with doing the dishes was that it interrupted her painting. She was just beginning to feel divine inspiration again and she longed to go to the basement, to her own special space that had been granted to her as a place to paint. She knew exactly what she needed to paint. She would start with a whitewash on the canvas. Then, she would mix cadmium blue with black and begin the painting at the bottom of the canvas with deep, heavy strokes. She could feel the inspiration bubbling in her gut, churning with each imagined brush stroke. The force of the churning worked its way into her brain, pulsing it with the visions and imagery that screamed to be put onto the canvas. She wanted to go there right now, right *now*, right *fucking now*. Fuck these stupid dishes and fuck the stupid women with whom she was supposed to be making 'nice.' She didn't give a rat's ass about her interactions with the other women. All she wanted to do was give in to the powerful forces telling her what to paint.

Elizabeth reacted anew to the water touching her hands, her beautiful painting hands. With her senses heightened, she could feel everything with which her fingers made contact, but she found it impossible to pull them away. She was frozen there, imbedded in the grip of the water. In an instant, she could feel the prickly jabs of bubbles as they touched and broke against her skin. Her left hand was touching a miniscule, soggy crust of bread, the mushy texture pressing against her fingers like raw hamburger. She dry heaved. Against the back of her right hand she could feel the rubbery edge of a fried egg. This time when she gagged, she could actually taste the bile building in the back of her throat and she swallowed it down. She looked into the sink and saw that her hands were immersed in the residual, mushy, brown shit left over from someone's Cocoa Puffs cereal. The immediate, overwhelming revulsion propelled her away from the sink. The force with which she pulled her hands from the sink flung the filthy water onto the counter and onto the floor. Streaks flew onto the cupboards and splashed back onto her. As she watched the water dropping all around her, her vision expanded to the dishes strewn from one end of the counter to the other. There were too many dishes. Too many dishes were on the counter, the table, the island, the stove, and the floor. There were dishes with rotting oranges, curdling cereal, and decaying bacon. Elizabeth's eyes shifted from the counter to the island to the table to the sink to the floor, from the counter to the island to the table to the sink to the floor. Then, she just stood there and stared, immobilized by her disgust with the filth. Fuck.

And suddenly Matron arrived. Elizabeth wasn't ready for her. Panic swelled in her throat as she glared at Matron. "Elizabeth?" Matron said. "Are you alright?" Elizabeth didn't know what to do. She couldn't focus her thoughts. She couldn't remember her plan. She couldn't think of a new one. She just wanted out of this room, out of the kitchen, out of the island trap, away from the water and the dishes.

Without a second thought, she allowed her psychologically conditioned self to take over. She grabbed the mug from the back of the sink, opened the faucet to splash water into it, grabbed the pills from Matron and took them. Really took them. She opened her mouth in disgust at Matron as she showed her the dark, cavernous cave into which the pills had slipped. Matron examined, cautiously smiled, and left.

Elizabeth remained rock-solid-still, staring again at the sink, the drained mug still clutched in her hand.

She stood. She stared. Her heart beat in her chest like a jackhammer.

She stood. She stared. The continued blasts from the jackhammer entered her brain and pounded against her ears, trying to get out.

She stood. She stared. Her throat constricted, growing tighter and tighter, squeezing the air right out of her. Then, like a shove from God, she felt the cool blast of air whooshing at her from behind as the Lesbian from London opened the front door and shouted, "I'm outta here!" The slam of the door as it closed shook the floor boards beneath Elizabeth's feet, jarring her, shaking the stiffness away. She blinked her eyes as if returning from a dream and she turned her head to look at the clock. It was 9:15. She'd just stood there that whole time, not thinking, not planning. Nothing. Shit!

Then she remembered—she had taken the pills. She grabbed at her throat as if the pressure from her hand could somehow hinder the pills from becoming assimilated into her body. She gagged again as she thought of the pills breaking down and being absorbed into her stomach. Could she wretch them out? Another dry heave formed in

Black Blood

her throat but she could not allow herself to perform the grotesque act of vomiting. She closed her eyes and shook her head back and forth with the strength of an animal caught in a trap. She needed a plan; she needed order. What could she do? Nothing. Just get the dishes done and get the fuck out of here. Don't think about the medicine. One entire dose of medication will not throw off your plan. Get the dishes done. She opened her eyes and approached the sink. With resolve to complete her task, she threw the mug into the sink, and reached for a set of tongs from the drawer. Using the tongs as an extension of her fingers, she manoeuvred it to the bottom of the sink, caught the plug between the pincers and pulled the plug up so the sink would drain of all its disgustingly filthy water. She turned on the hot water tap and let it pour into the emptying sink and down into the drain. Carefully, so her hands did not touch any water or the remnants of any food, she lifted each dish and placed it under the surge of the waterfall flowing from the Delta tap. Dish after dish, she watched in disgust as the water forced the food off and pushed it into the awaiting drain. She piled these semi-washed dishes onto the draining tray, grabbed a dry towel and wiped her hands.

She ground the towel into the palms of her hands to wipe away the wetness. She shaped it around each finger and squeezed it there, grinding the towel's stiff surface into every wrinkle and every crevice of every digit of each hand to soak up the moisture. She wound it around her wrists, circling them again and again to ensure they were dry. Then, with the flair of a bull fighter and his cape, she snapped the towel across the table and the counter, flicking the crumbs onto the floor. When she moved to the stove, she spied a bowl still full of thick, chunky oatmeal, just left sitting there. The oatmeal looked like vomit and Elizabeth dry heaved again. She could not touch the bowl with her bare hands, so she placed the towel over and between her hands, as if preparing to reach into an oven for a hot pan. She cautiously lifted the dish up off the counter and, gagging again, she stepped on the lever that flipped open the top of the garbage so she could deposit the dish directly into the bin. She wasn't cleaning that shit. Her hands would not touch any of that slime.

Once the lid of the garbage can dropped shut, she used her hip to push the island back into the centre of the kitchen. Holding it steady with her hands still enshrined in the towel, she locked it into place. Then, leaving the rest of her responsibilities behind, she threw the towel onto the counter and retreated down the steps of the basement, to her place of sanctuary and sanity.

Exhausted and shaking, she slunk onto her painting stool. She placed both hands on her lap and sat very, very still. Staring at the easel in front of her, she allowed the smell of turpentine to fill her nostrils and cleanse her olfactory nerves of the wretched smell of the kitchen. She inhaled the smell of the oils, too, mixed with the mustiness of the basement. She continued to breathe in and out, slowly, methodically, until all she could smell was painting.

Black Blood

Doctor Almighty had taught her to do this breathing exercise many years ago. In and out. In and out. Slowly. Methodically. Breathe. Her heart stopped pounding. Her shoulders relaxed and she took a deep, cleansing breath.

Once she felt calmed, and her nose was filled only with the smell of her own space, she picked up a filbert brush and rolled the smooth, wooden handle through her fingers. She could feel its warm, yellow energy pass from the polished handle into her fingertips. She raised the brush to her cheek and ran the sable bristles from her ear to her chin and back again. Over and over, back and forth, up and down. And breathing. In and out. The bristles were warm and caressing. She felt the sexual tingle create gooseflesh on her face and down onto her neck. A tightness formed in her groin and a low moan escaped from her throat as she closed her eyes and tilted her head back to rest on the wall behind her. Breathe. In and out. In and out.

She allowed her arms to fall back onto her lap as she sat with her eyes closed. She continued to inhale slowly through her nose and exhale softly through her mouth. She envisioned herself in Dr. Anderson's room, stretched out and relaxed, listening to his quiet, rolling words. "Take a deep, cleansing breath in," he'd lull. "Slowly release it through your mouth. Control your breathing, Elizabeth. That's the way. Gently in. And out. In. And out." He paused his lullaby as she opened her mouth and let the air leave her. "Good. Deep breath in," he'd instruct again. "You are thinking only of the pure air entering into your body. The air coming in through your nose is cleansing and soothing. It travels down your throat making it cool and fresh." Another pause. Elizabeth continued to envision her session with Doctor Almighty, breathing deeply and relaxing.

He speaks to her memories. "Feel the pressure on your chest as the cool air enters your body." He would watch her, making sure she was taking the steady, deep breaths he demanded. "It travels to your lungs, filling them with fresh, cleansing air. Inhale. Good. Your lungs inhale the cleansing air into each of the thousands of tiny air pockets." He gave her time to envision the air molecules entering her nose, travelling down into her lungs, and scrubbing away at each of the air pockets like miniature loofah pads. "The air is cleaning them. Cleansing them, creating a clean environment to which the blood can come to be cleansed, to become clean." Another pause as he studied her, watching her concentrate on expanding her abdomen up as far it could go, inflated like a puffer fish. "Your blood absorbs the oxygen from the cleansing air and becomes bright red. Bright red: the colour of oxygenated blood, of cleansed blood, of cleaned blood, of re-nourished blood, clean blood that is ready to travel to the rest of your body for your health. For your wellness. Clean blood. Pure blood. Red blood."

After several minutes of watching her inhale and exhale, he'd quietly interrupt her with the gentle question, "Elizabeth. What colour are the cells?"

And she'd respond sleepily, "Red. The cells are red. All red."

– 4 –

Cursed

I am twelve. For two days I've had a belly ache. I feel kinda sick to my stomach, but the pain is lower down than in my belly. I kinda feel like I gotta poop, but that's not it either. I went to school Thursday and Friday, but today, Saturday, I don't wanna get up. Sometimes, on Saturdays, Nana lets me stay in bed 'cause I don't have to go to school and it lets her do her cleaning in solitude. So, I have decided to just stay in bed until my stomach feels better.

I wonder if I have a stomach ache because of something I ate. I make my own meals now and do all of the grocery shopping. Nana has gotten too old to do this chore. She doesn't go outside of the house much anymore so, on Saturdays, I take her pushcart to the A & P and get what we need. Nana makes a list of the foods she wants, and I add things onto the list that I need. I need things for my lunches like pudding cups and bananas and cold meat. I eat a lot of cereal and canned soups for my other meals, so I make sure we have lots of Cheerios and milk. I wonder if the milk I had on my cereal last night was starting to go sour. Maybe that's why my belly hurts. I'll get good, fresh milk when I go to the grocery store later today.

I begin to think about what food I need to buy for my lunches this week. As I begin to think about bologna and fruit cups, my belly protests with a squeezing cramp; the belly ache has taken away my appetite this morning and has even made me nauseous. I can't think about food right now so I just lie in bed and listen to the swoosh, swoosh, swoosh sound as Nana draws the scrub brush in circles on the kitchen floor. The kitchen will be spotless now, so I won't be able to eat in there until lunch time—Nana won't let me dirty-up the kitchen until 11:45. That's OK, I think to myself, I don't need breakfast. I feel so crappy that I'll just go back to sleep. I roll over, facing away from the bedroom door, and grab the blankets to pull them tight around my belly. I drift off into a half-sleep that is filled with dreams and images. I dream I am sitting on the toilet, trying to poop. The cramps in my dream are as real as if I were fully awake. When I fall into a deeper sleep, I see myself sitting in a nice warm tub, my buttocks and thighs warmed by the water. The faucet is dripping into the tub. Plunk. Plunk. Plunk. I extend my hand and turn the tap righty-tighty. It doesn't do any good. It still drips. Plunk. Plunk. Plunk. I try to turn the tap tighter, but now the water gushes out from it, roaring as it cascades into the tub. The water is hot and sticky. It's burning my legs and my private area. I want out of the tub, and knowing that I am dreaming, I pull myself away from the nightmare and open my eyes.

Although I am awake, I continue to hear the cascading water. I listen closer, trying to figure out what the sound is, until I realize it is the sound of the vacuum cleaner. Nana has brought it from the main floor, plunk, plunk, plunking it against the stairs as she carried it up. The cascading sound of water in my dream is actually the sound of the vacuum cleaner as Nana performs the daily cleaning ritual in her bedroom. I relax a little, knowing that I recognize the sound, but then I sense that something else is wrong. Something feels unusual, and I freeze. The bed feels wet. It feels wet and warm between my legs, just like in my dream. Did I pee? Did I have an accident? I try to move but my gut hurts so bad that the pain goes all the way around to my back and I am immobilized. I have never had pain like this before and I am scared. In all the years that I've lived with Nana, I've never, ever been really sick. Sure, I've had a few colds and the chicken pox, but I haven't ever been sick enough to be in pain.

The vacuum cleaner suddenly switches off and I hear Nana coming to my room. I am overwhelmed with fear. What do I tell her? I can't tell her I've had an accident! My God! I'm twelve years old—way too old for an accident. I cannot begin to imagine what she would do to me if she found out I've had an accident.

Quickly, I form a plan. I will lie perfectly still and pretend to be asleep. When she comes into my room, she'll see my sleeping body, retreat from my room, and leave me alone.

Lorrie Werden

Then, I will get up, put the wet sheets into the hamper, take them downstairs and start the laundry. I do the laundry now anyway. Nana finds it too hard to go down and up the crooked basement stairs so, when I turned ten, she taught me how to do the laundry. I learned how to sort the clothes and how to pre-treat them before they go into the machine. She taught me how to shake out each article of clothing before putting it into the dryer, and how to take the clothes out of the dryer before the buzzer goes off and to hang them up quickly so they don't wrinkle. She even taught me how to fold towels and fitted sheets so they all fit properly in the linen closet. She will not think it strange that I am taking my hamper down to the basement. It will be an expectation.

I clench my eyes tight and listen for Nana's arrival. Although my heart is pounding, I know I must keep my breath slow and steady. If I'm breathing too fast, she'll know I'm awake, and she'll demand that I get up and start my chores right away. I can't do that. I can't get up—she'll see that I've wet the bed—so I just lie very, very still, controlling my breathing. Nana's footsteps get closer to my door and I can hear her hand on the doorknob. It clunks as she turns it and I can hear the soft rubbing of the hinges as they allow the door to ease open. Nana does not come into my room, but I can feel her eyes on me, watching me. I breathe slowly and my body remains motionless. I count my breaths. One—in/out. Two—in/out. Three—in/out. Four—in/out. Five—in/out. Go away, I will her. Go away. I hear the hinges swoosh as she closes the door, the striker latches as it finds its place in the door frame, and I know she is gone.

I hesitantly move my hand toward my bum. I need to feel how badly I have wet the bed. My fingertips travel to my waist and make their way under my hip, between my nightie and the fitted sheet. It's dry here. I move my hand to feel the sheet under my thigh. Dry here, too. Maybe I didn't wet the bed at all. I don't feel the warmth or wetness anymore in my panties, so maybe it was just the dream. I cautiously push the covers away from my body and, using my elbow as a prop, I lift myself up into a half sitting position. I look at the sheets. Nothing. No wetness, no pee.

Relieved, I swing my legs over the side of the bed, but I get a cramp in my gut and cannot quite make it to standing. As this cramp continues to grip me, it feels like it is pushing a big ball of pee through me. I need to get to the bathroom before I really do have an accident.

I hobble to my door and quietly enter the hallway. I can see Nana dusting her room and, as I slip past her bedroom door, I can see she has already stripped her bed and the laundry hamper, already clutching her dirty sheets, is waiting for me to carry them downstairs. Perfect. Even though they are not wet with pee, I'll just add my sheets to hers and carry them down together. I go into the bathroom, quickly hoist my nightie up to my waist, pull down my undies, and plunk myself down on the toilet.

Then I see it. The red splotch on my underwear. I know what is happening, we learned about it at school. I'm beginning my menses. I didn't know, though, that when the blood came out of my body it would hurt. I start to pee and I can feel a different wet stickiness come out of the other part of my private area. The vagina, I remember it's called. I can hear the lady from the Health Unit say, "If an egg is not fertilized, the blood comes away from the uterus once a month. This is your period. It is also called menstruation, or menses. It is a perfectly normal part of what a girl's body goes through to become a woman. Don't be afraid to share the beginning of your menses with the women who love you. They will understand exactly what you are going through. They will also suggest which feminine hygiene products are best for you to use at the time of onset of your period. This is a wonderful life event to share with your mother, so don't be afraid to talk to her."

Later, in the playground, after our 'talk' was completed, some of the girls were in a group, swapping stories.

"I got my period in the summer."

"I got mine last year. I was really young, but mom says I'm way more mature for my age."

Some boys are eavesdropping. "You're on the rag," they chanted. "You're on the rag."

"Red sails in the sunset."

"Pandora's box is broken."

I had never heard these things before and I didn't know what they meant.

Black Blood

And now I don't know what to say to Nana. I know I need feminine hygiene products, but I am embarrassed to tell her. The only thing I can do is just continue to sit on the toilet.

I hear Nana go downstairs. I can hear her moving around, cleaning the living room. Since it's my job now to clean my own room, her time spent cleaning has greatly decreased, leaving her more time to watch the television. Since she found religion, she still watches Midday Mass, *but her religious viewing has expanded to watching* Prayer Palace, Crystal Cathedral, *and* PTL Club. *That's what she does now. She watches TV and waits for divine intervention.*

After a very long while, I hear her move again. This time I can hear her coming up the stairs. She reaches the bathroom door and knocks. "Elizabeth Devereux, what are you doing in there?"

"Nana?" I call back. "I'm sick." It's the only thing I can think of to say. She opens the door and sees me sitting on the toilet. I can see in her eyes that she's trying to figure out what's wrong with me. If I were standing over the toilet, she would know that I'd been sick to my stomach, but just sitting here on the toilet, I can tell she thinks I have diarrhea. I pull my nightie up and away from my undies and I pull them forward, away from my legs, so she can see the red.

Immediately, her body stiffens. "You've got the curse," she says. "I don't have anything here for that. You're too young for that." She's panicking now. "You'll have to go to the store to get something. I don't have anything here." She begins to wring her hands. "You'll have to go. I can't go." She turns her back to me and starts to move away from the bathroom door to make a retreat into her bedroom. From behind the closed bedroom door she calls, "I'll make you a pad for now, but you'll have to go to the store. You'll have to buy something for that."

I stare through the void that has been left by the still-opened bathroom door and I can feel a big, fat tear roll down my cheek. I suddenly realize, and understand, that I have no mother with which to share my entry into womanhood. I also understand that I will be solely responsible for my own care and for finding which feminine hygiene product is best for me.

But worse than that, is what Nana said. She said I've got the curse. In my twelve year old head, that translates to: I am cursed.

– 5 –

Doctor Almighty

At 9:55, Elizabeth's watch beeped to remind her of the meeting with Doctor Almighty. Groggily, she pulled herself into consciousness. She took one last cleansing breath and realized her hissy fit with the dishes was finished. She felt better now, rested and relaxed. She stood up, closed her eyes, and stretched her arms far above her head, inhaling the wonderful smells of the basement into her lungs and her body. She exhaled and opened her eyes. She checked her watch again: 9:57. She'd better go. She didn't want to be late for her appointment. She didn't need to go to her room to get her blue book. She hadn't written in it yet today and, if Doctor Almighty wanted to know what had happened this morning, she would just simply tell him that she had experienced an anxiety attack when she was washing the dishes. He would say something like, "Describe the incident that precipitated the attack." She would tell him that she wasn't sure what had precipitated it, but to cope with it, she had just reached into her extraordinary repertoire of cognitive behaviour management techniques, and pulled out a deep muscle relaxation exercise that she implemented to calm herself. He'd love to hear that shit. She made her way up the staircase, down the hall, and into Dr. Anderson's anteroom.

Elizabeth hated the anteroom. Institutional beige paint was slathered on the walls and the cracking tiles beneath her feet were cold and unwelcoming, and today, after just emerging from a panic attack, the room seemed even more daunting.

The anteroom was part of the Matrons' domain, theirs to organize and clean. It was, therefore, plain and cold. It was sterile. It was worse than a hospital ward. It was certainly worse than Six E. There were no magazines to read, no artwork to critique, no brochures to peruse, no cutesy pictures drawn by any of the Matrons' grandchildren to make you feel relaxed and say, "Oh, my. Isn't this pleasant." Not even a fucking coffee table on which to rest her feet. There was nothing in here that would need the Matron's attention and, most specifically, there was nothing in this room that could agitate, instigate, or inspire any poor woman who had to sit here waiting for Doctor Almighty to rescue her from this room. Except, of course, the room itself.

Elizabeth sat down on the 1970's low, angular, plastic couch and pondered her existence in the anteroom around her. Her first thought was that 'anti-room' was an incredibly stupid name for a room. An *anti*-room. She understood the spelling difference, but how the hell can it be called an anti-room? It's a room against other rooms? Is it the same as anti-abortionists who are against abortions, and anti-terrorists who are against terrorists? Stupid, stupid name.

Her second thought, as she sat in the anteroom, was that she felt very uncomfortable here. It wasn't because the couch was hard or because the floor was cold beneath her feet, it was because she felt trapped in here. She knew she could simply exit the room and go back into the hall, but that wasn't the correct order of how things should proceed. The correct order was for her to come into the 'anti-room', wait, Doctor Almighty would come and let her into his room, she would have her session with him, and then she would leave by the other door that exited through Matron's office. If she were to interrupt this pattern, if she were to leave now, for instance, she might miss her session. She didn't know if Dr. Anderson would come looking for her, or if he would be angry that she left, but it would be very bad if she left the room, so she stayed where she was, staring at the walls that seemed to be closing in on her.

Her line of sight went to the farthest corner away from her. She stared at it momentarily, until her eyes began to dart, on their own, from one corner of the room to another, from the floor to the ceiling, and back again. Over and over. With each sweep of her eyes, the distance from the one corner of the room to the other, and from the floor to the ceiling, got smaller and smaller. Her toes began to jump anxiously inside her socks as her eyes continued to burn the edges of the shrinking room. Her heart began pounding in her ears. She wanted to be out of here. She didn't want to look at the 'anti-room' any more. She thought, "This *is* an anti-room." Anti-welcoming, anti-relaxing, anti-pleasant, anti-everything. And with each thought of how anti-welcoming this room was, how anti-relaxing this room was, how anti-pleasant this room was, a heavy, dank, sad fabric of 'anti' was wrapping around her, pushing her torso lower and lower toward her knees, crushing her like an anti-rock, pushing her into sadness. The weight of the sadness was making it difficult to breathe. She needed to inhale, to catch her breath. She had to get rid of the anti-cloak so she could breathe. She stood abruptly and wrenched her shoulders to shun the heaviness of the constricting anti-cloak.

Her breathing quickened and before she would allow another panic attack to overcome her, she quickly turned her body toward the wall beside her and focused her attention on a tiny crack she could just barely eke out in the paint. She put her nose against the crack and cupped her hands at her eyes, squeezing the sides of her face together. Not only did this block out her vision of the anti-room, but it allowed her to glare into the crack.

Pushing the existence of the anti-room out of her thoughts, she forced her eyes to examine the crack so deeply that she could see past the small fissure in the paint, and gaze right into the cracked wall itself. What she saw in the cracked plaster was absolutely beautiful. She saw before her an elaborate piece of art. Elizabeth could see each tiny piece of gravel that was the plaster's composite, and she could see the multitude of tiny grains of sand that filled the spaces between the bits of gravel. There were millions of them creating long, flowing edges of, what looked like, the beach. Miles and miles of white, warm sand, its beauty gently rubbing her nose and hands like the little loofah sponges used to cleanse her lungs. This thought calmed her. Her breathing slowed and her toes stopped twitching. Her breathing became steady; her heartbeat slowed. She felt better now as she stared at the wall.

Wanting to capture this feeling of security, she squeezed her eyelids closer together and pushed her nose so close to the wall that the tip of it was bent toward her cheek. Her eyes continued to burrow further into the plaster and delved into the drywall behind it. She could see the infinite, miniscule fibres that held the sheet rock together. And she could see the colours. Every infinite, miniscule fibre that she could see glowed with a rainbow of colours: bright, shining, illuminating colours. She found solace staring into the wall and would have been quite content to remain as she was, but she could not stop her eyes from piercing through the colours to see the hollow space beyond the sheet of drywall. She could see clearly through the wall, past the white electrical wire stapled to a stud, through the opposing drywall, through its plaster and through its paint to see the light of Doctor Almighty's office. She was amazed that she could see that far into the room, but when she was illuminated by the sunlight shining in through his office windows, she was instantly consumed with embarrassment. How dare she go into his office uninvited? She sucked her vision back into her eye sockets and jumped back from the wall, startled at what she had done and what she had seen.

In disbelief, she shook her head and sat back down on the sofa. She placed her hands over her eyes and rubbed them harshly until all she could see behind her closed eyelids was pitch black. With her eyes still closed, she lowered her hands, intertwined her fingers, and placed them in her lap. Slowly, she opened her eyes and tried to focus on a small spot of paint that was on a cracked tile directly between her two feet. Although she was still in embarrassed awe at being able to see through the wall into Doctor Almighty's room, watching the spot allowed her to feel more grounded and more at peace.

Then, the door opened, and Doctor Almighty invited her in.

Elizabeth snapped to attention and realized that the opened door to Dr. Anderson's office was her way to flee the anti-room. She slipped past Doctor Almighty and stepped quickly into his visiting room. With one deep and prolonged inhale and exhale of peaceful air, Elizabeth was immediately at ease and felt calmed and welcomed.

Elizabeth loved this room. It was the complete opposite of the anti-room. Opposite, she thought, of anti. This then, she reasoned, since it is the opposite of anti, must be the for-room. No. She corrected her thoughts. Not the for-room.

Black Blood

The pro-room! Doctor Almighty should call this room his *pro*-room, not his visiting room. He has an anti-room and a pro-room, she mused. A pro-room for the pros. She smiled at the ingenuity of the thoughts that were now bubbling in her head. Everyone who comes to this halfway house is a pro: the prostitutes, the professionals, the proliferates, the probationers, the probed, and the prodded. All pros. Right here, right now, in Elizabeth's brain, this was officially the pro-room. A room where you go to project, profess, progress, and propose new treatments. Pro, pro, pro, pro. Her grin turned to a giggle and she caught Dr. Anderson looking quizzically at her. She lowered her head and bit her bottom lip. She swallowed the spit that had accumulated under her tongue during her excitement of the pro words. Another deep breath. Inhale. Exhale. Calm.

She raised her head and noticed that Dr. Anderson had seated himself. Taking in the vision of the doctor in his chair, Elizabeth also took time to see the surrounding room. She could not help but be drawn to the sun streaming in from the series of glass windows all along the south wall. It reminded her that she had been an uninvited intruder a few minutes ago, and her embarrassment was renewed. She shifted her eyes toward Doctor Almighty, suspecting that he might say something about her invasion, but he seemed more interested in his notebook than in her momentary intrusion, so Elizabeth returned her eyes back toward the windows. The sun shone brightly enough that no other lights were actually needed in this room, but the good doctor had a table lamp that illuminated the head of the sofa where Elizabeth would sit, and another small lamp situated on his desk. The desk, by its great width, clearly marked, as a gated wall might mark an entry into a mansion, the area between it and the windows, as Doctor Almighty's private territory. The desk was made of a deep, dark wood, mahogany she thought, and its glistening surface reflected the heat of the sun into the entire room. It smelled of Lemon Pledge. If you bent over the desk, you could see your reflection in its shiny surface, your face darkened by the colour of the wood and slightly distorted by its grain.

Combined with the tang of Lemon Pledge, Elizabeth could smell the leather from the various collections of bound books that lined the shelves to her left, and she wondered if this was what an uncle's study would smell like. Someone's uncle, like on the television or in the movies. An uncle wearing a smoking jacket and puffing mightily on a pipe. Elizabeth breathed deeply again to ingrain the smell into her nostrils.

"Elizabeth?" Dr. Anderson's voice interrupted her thoughts. "Please. Have a seat." Elizabeth looked at him. Although Dr. Anderson's extended hand was an invitation for her to sit on the rounded couch, her eyes travelled past the couch to the series of frames hanging along the entire width of the west wall. Toward the south end, and closer to his designated private property area, were his degrees and diplomas that plastered his name all over the wall. Big, sturdy, expensive, wood frames protected the flimsy pieces of merit, encasing forever Dr. Anderson's exorbitantly priced journey of learning and discovery. On the wall directly above the couch were much smaller frames that proffered letters of gratitude. There were letters from patients and their families, and from mental health organizations and support groups, all thanking him for his help with their struggles. There was even a letter from the Dean of the University of Montreal's Ecole Polytechnique, thanking him for his counselling and grief management services after the massacre in 1989. Elizabeth walked over to the couch, but rather than sitting on it, she leaned over it, one hand bracing the back, as her knees bent onto the cushions for support. She leaned into the wall and ran the fingers of her free hand along that particular frame. It was made of cheap, painted plastic. Huh. Helping countless people deal with the deaths of 14 lives was only worth the cost of a dollar store frame. Her fingertips rested on the frame and she held her position there as her mind travelled to images of the massacre. She was only two when it happened, so she had no solid recollection of the event, but she had learned about it in high school and she remembered the name, Marc Lepine.

In her mind's eye, she could easily imagine the scene. She could see the bloodiness of it. All that blood spewing from the bodies of the young women who were killed. Blood on the floors. Blood on desks and carpets. Blood that could never be washed out. Blood everywhere. She concentrated so hard on the redness of the blood that it became darker, deeper, turning black, and numbing her brain. She was staring at the framed letter, but she saw only blackness, as if her eyes were closed. She stopped breathing and held her breath for as long as she could. When she eventually had to gulp for air, the blackness disappeared and the vision of blood was gone. With a shudder, she turned and sat down. She had not been there in 1989, but her vision of the devastation created by that one man was as clear to her as if she had been one of the surviving women.

She blinked several times then, and focused her attention on Dr. Anderson while she inhaled a deep, calming breath. She stared at Dr. Anderson. She needed to be here, in the present, with Dr. Anderson. She actually smiled at him, and waited.

After a few minutes of continued writing, he looked at her and returned the smile. Dr. Anderson's face was warm and familiar to Elizabeth. The half glasses that were perched near the end of his pointy nose threatened to fall off if he moved too quickly, but he never moved fast enough for them to be hit by gravity. His movements always seemed so controlled and fluid, as if he were moving in a lava lamp. His balding head was highlighted from the glow of the lamp near the couch, and the light illuminated a forehead that seemed to go on forever. The remaining fringe of greying hair was long enough that it swept across the collar of his hip-length sherwani shirt. He sat in his brown leather chair with his legs crossed in the lotus position, the bottom of his bare feet shiny against his khaki pants. He was a combination hippy, grandpa, friend, and authority figure all rolled into one.

Elizabeth liked him. When he smiled, thousands of lines careened out from the corners of his eyes, like rays from the sun. His mouth opened wide when he smiled and showed teeth that were quite crooked and deeply yellowed from years of smoking. Elizabeth closed her eyes and inhaled deeply again. He did not, however, smell of smoke. He smelled of sand and water. He smelled fresh and clean. In this room with him, Elizabeth felt safe and sheltered, as if she was in the protection of the Almighty God Himself. She could relax here and allow Dr. Anderson's lulling voice to pull from her all the right words, all the right phrases, and all the right answers to his conjectured questions.

"Well, Elizabeth," he started, "tell me about your movements after our session yesterday."

Doctor Almighty always knew what things to say to invoke people to talk to him. He never asked stupid questions like the emergency room, on-call doctors did. They never knew what questions to ask her. "Are you taking any drugs?" they'd ask. Hell, no! Try to figure that one out, boys. No, she wasn't taking any drugs—it was lack of taking drugs that was making her behave this way! "Are you aware of where you are, Miss Devereux?" She knew perfectly well where she was and she also knew that she just wanted to be the fuck out of there. She never went to the hospital under her own free will. She was usually dragged into the ER room at four in the morning by bristly little men in their EMS uniforms under the direction of the stiff-assed bitch from down the hall who had called the police to tell them that Elizabeth's creative energy (OK, her screaming) was keeping her from getting the precious beauty sleep she needed.

Of course, once in the ER room, she would barricade herself under the gurney or behind the tray of bandages, and they'd back off. She was a nut job best suited for a psych, not for these lowly medical doctors who weren't properly trained to handle mental illness cases. This one, they agreed, was for Doctor Almighty. They'd place a call to him. If they were lucky, he'd answer their call immediately and suggest the right kind of medication to give to her. They'd hold her down and give her the injection and she'd calm down for them. Then she'd wait for Doctor Almighty to come and rescue her.

If they weren't lucky though, they'd get his answering machine and then be stuck with her for hours as her displays of mania unfolded. They'd put her in a private room with a security guard as sentry, and try to block out her verbal ravings and shrill screams. But then, Doctor Almighty would come and he'd talk to her. He could ask her questions without even putting his words into the form of a query. He'd put forth a phrase, a sentence, or a speech fragment, to gently prod answers from her. This formal procedure skirted the issues, but he was always able to lead her into giving him the answers he wanted and, from her responses, he knew which meds to give to her to bring her down.

And Elizabeth knew, right now, that when he said, "Tell me about your movements after our session yesterday morning," he was trying to determine if, in fact, she was on the right dose of medications.

– 6 –

Gone

I am sixteen years old and have been in bed for three days. Nana has called up the stairs to me today, but I have not answered her. I just haven't been able to. I answered her yesterday and the day before that when she asked if I was sick. "Yes," I yelled back and then yelled back again, "No," to her question of needing anything. But today, I just can't answer.

In the late afternoon, I can hear her ascending the staircase. It is the first time in three years that Nana has climbed the stairs. She'd gotten too old, she'd said, to 'do' the stairs anymore, so she began sleeping on the couch. She'd had a plumber and an electrician come to the house, and they transformed the closet under the staircase into a two-piece bathroom for her. Once she had a toilet within walking distance, she stopped coming upstairs at all. Soon, the entire living room was her bedroom.

Lorrie Werden

But today, she has reason to come up the stairs. I am definitely ill—there is definitely something wrong with me. I haven't eaten or bathed since last Friday. I didn't get groceries on Saturday. I haven't done any laundry—mine or hers. I missed school today, and in the past three days, I've gotten out of bed only four, quick times, to relieve myself so I didn't have to wash my sheets. She's coming up the stairs today to find out when I'll go get the groceries, when I'll do her laundry, and when I'll help her clean the kitchen.

She quietly enters my room and crosses to my bed. I can feel in an instant that something is different. Somehow, she is not my same Nana. Maybe the excursion up the stairs has knocked the wind out of her, or maybe her advanced age is making her softer, kinder to me somehow; but whatever has happened, she doesn't bark at me to get out of bed. She doesn't glare at me with her Prussian blue eyes that feel like daggers plunging into my soul. She doesn't hurt me at all. I want to roll over, to look into her face to see what has happened, but I just can't. I want to sit up and tell her that I'm sad and that I really just need a hug, but she wouldn't understand that. She'd be happier if I told her that I'm fine and that I'll get up now to do the laundry, but that would be a lie. I can't get up. I am positively stuck to my bed. My body weighs thousands of tons and has trapped me against my mattress. Nana moves around the bed so she can see my face. I am so consumed with the weight of my body that I can't even turn my eyes to look at her. I just continue to stare at the wall. She bends over me and wipes my hair away from my face. Her touch is soft and gentle and I am so overcome by this sudden act of kindness that a tear trickles out of my eye and rolls across the bridge of my nose, plopping onto my pillow.

"Elizabeth?" she says softly. I cannot answer her. My mind cannot get the words to form in my head, to travel to my mouth, to be formed by my tongue, then be pushed out by my lungs. I just don't have the energy. So, instead, I just stare at the wall.

Nana draws her hand away from my face and brings it to her own face, covering her mouth. I can hear her say ever so quietly, "Oh, God, no. Please. No." She stares at me for a few more minutes, then turns, and leaves my room. I hear her descending the stairs, going back to the living room, and I can hear her making a telephone call. She is speaking in hushed tones and her words are garbled and unintelligible. Then it is quiet. Nana does not even turn on the television.

I do not go to sleep, but I am certainly not awake. I am just somewhere else, somewhere deep within myself, searching for a way home, and wishing that Nana was still here with me, gently touching my face. Somehow, I know if Nana could just touch me again, that simple contact would be enough to pull me from this crushing weight.

When it is dark outside, Father Michaels comes to the house. He speaks to my Nana for a few minutes, the hall light comes on, he climbs the stairs, and comes into my room. As dead as I feel, the shame of having Father Michaels see me like this is much stronger. I need to sit up. I need to look presentable for Father Michaels. The most I can muster, though, is to turn over onto my back and wipe the drool from the side of my mouth.

"Elizabeth," he says as he props himself against my window sill. "Your grandmother called me and asked if I'd come over. May I talk to you for a few minutes?" I am able to nod my head.

"She says you're feeling a bit under the weather. Are you sick, Elizabeth?" I don't know how to answer. I'm not sick like I have a cold or the flu, but I don't feel right. I feel sad. I am so sad that sorrow has swept over me like a weighted blanket and is sucking me onto my bed. I am sad because I have been dumped by my boyfriend. I am able to whisper to Father Michaels that Trevor MacDougall dumped me and I am sad.

And Father Michaels smiles.

"Ah. So it's a bit of boyfriend trouble, then, eh? Well, the best cure for that is to get up and get going again. I'm sure you'll be fine in a few days. Young love can be tough," he continues, "but you're a lovely young woman—I know you'll have many more boys knocking down your door soon enough. You just be a good girl and continue to ask the Virgin Mary for her guidance. I'll light a candle for you and everything will be fine." He crosses to the end of my bed, taps the bump that is my foot, and says, "Be a good girl now, Elizabeth, and get up for your grandmother. She's worried about you."

I hear him descend the stairs and speak in hushed tones to Nana. I can hear him laugh and I know he is patting her hand to comfort her. When I hear him leave, and the front door closes behind him, I turn back to the wall. The light

Black Blood

from the hallway continues to shine into my room and it illuminates the tiny purple flowers on the wallpaper. I don't know why, but I can suddenly feel the grief with which my body has been stricken. I remember that Trevor dumped me and I recall all of the awful things he said to me about the black cells, but I was only trying to share my experience with him. I just wanted him to help me get the black cells out of my hand. He didn't understand what the black cells were, and I had no words to explain them to him. I told him that sometimes, when I got really upset or scared, my body makes black cells that overpower the red ones. The black cells are really heavy and if I don't push them out, they get so heavy in my hand that it just won't move. I told him this was why I couldn't touch him. My hand couldn't touch his hardened cock because of the black cells.

"You're whacked," he said. "You'll let me fuck you, but you won't give me a hand job?"

"No," I cried, "it's not that I don't want to touch you. I just can't. Please," I begged him, "help me rub them out." I was grinding the base of my left thumb with the fingers of my right hand, rubbing it to try to break up the collection of black cells that had accumulated there, but they were fused too tightly together to scatter them.

I'd felt them starting to collect when we were at the movie and I'd been able to grind out a few of them, but when we got back to the car, drove out of town to a back country road, and started making out, more of them had gathered. When he grabbed my hand and placed it on the bulge in his jeans, the heat created more black cells, and I'd jerked my hand away as if I'd touched hot coals. He was offended.

"Oh, come on," he said. "You don't want to leave me hurting, do you?" He pulled my face close to his and enshrouded my lips with his. We were kissing. He was groaning as he pushed his tongue into my mouth. I wanted to respond. I wanted to feel the heat rise in my crotch like it had last week. I wanted him to touch my breasts, my thighs, my pussy. I wanted to climb into the back seat with him and let him push up my Catholic skirt, pull down my underwear, and grind himself into me. I really did. But I just couldn't pull my attention away from the black cells.

"Please," I moaned as I pulled myself away from his grasp. "Please, I just need to go home. I need to get into the shower to wash the cells away. Please." I looked at him with begging eyes, expecting him to comfort me, to help me, to understand my fear. Instead, he pushed me away in disgust, his hand heavy on my shoulder as I fell back against the car door. The impact of my upper back striking the hard door sent a burst of pain down into my arm. I screamed in alarm.

"You asshole," I yelled. "Now there will be more cells!" Tears began forming in my eyes as I became acutely aware of the number of black cells growing in my hand. I lifted my leg toward Trevor and began kicking him with my left foot. "You fucking asshole," I repeated as I pummelled him. "You've made it worse."

Trevor raised his arm across his body to protect himself from my attack and when I continued to assail him, he thrust his arm toward me, sending my leg into the dashboard. I sat up and he hit me again. This time, my body was forced into the car door and my head hit the glass. The pain was so intense that it recoiled me to a little ball on the seat of his car.

"Fuckin' hit at me, you stupid bitch." Trevor started the car. "Fuckin' black cells. You are fucked. Fucked in the fucking head." He put the car in reverse, pulled a u-turn, and drove back into the city towards my house. His tirade continued all the way home and all I could do was whither into myself, away from his anger, away from his words, even away from the black cells. I wanted to escape from him, from his hurtful words, from the car, from this moment, and from my life. The only way I could do that was to allow a black blanket to envelope me as I whimpered in fear and pain.

By the time he screeched to a halt in front of my house, I was very quiet. I was wrapped up so tightly in my little black ball, that I was numb.

"Get out," I heard Trevor growl. "Get the fuck out of my car." With the help of his foot pushing on my ass, I was able to get out of the car and onto the grass. Before I had a chance to close the door, Trevor drove off, leaving me curled up near the sidewalk, enveloped by the blackness.

I don't know how it happened, but somehow I managed to get up and walk in through the front door of my house. I said goodnight to Nana, got upstairs, stripped from my clothes, got into my nightgown, and climbed into bed.

Lorrie Werden

All that effort to get Trevor to take me home so I could shower to get rid of the black cells—and now I didn't need it. Somehow, the few black cells had been erased from my hand.

They were gone. But now—so was I.

– 7 –

Confessions

Elizabeth tensed as she sorted through the thoughts that suddenly invaded her head. She didn't want to discuss her medications with Dr. Anderson. She knew that reducing her medications could make the black cells come again and she drew to mind each of the days when she had slipped some of her medication down the sink. She evaluated her ability to function since she began self-medicating, and her conclusion was positive. She was still capable of completing the dishwashing task, even when the water was as vile as vomit, and her social interactions with the women and the Matrons had been appropriate. She felt really good about her progress. She had found an acceptable mix of random medication and inspiration, and looked forward to being at home where she would not need social niceties at all, and where she could just focus on her painting.

Lorrie Werden

She held her left thumb with her other hand and squeezed it. There were no dark pulses in her hand. Nope. No black cells. Elizabeth relaxed a little. Chill, she scolded herself. The black cells haven't been a problem and that was not what Doctor Almighty had asked her to describe. He didn't ask her either, about the panic attack (that was *not* brought on by the black cells) so she didn't need to address what happened this morning, and she could just tell him about last night without even mentioning today's panic attack. She just had to tell him about last night, not this morning. *Not* this morning. She paused for a moment, then took a deep breath. It was not a cleansing breath, it was just a deep gulp of air so she could begin her speech. She recalled what she had written in her journal and began to articulate her reflections of last night.

"Yesterday, after I retired from your office, I went to the basement." She recited the safe, comfortable words as if she were reading them directly from her blue book, "While there, I washed all of my brushes at the cast iron sink, dried them carefully on paper towels, and returned them to their container. I selected a new canvas and placed it on the easel. I'm not sure, as of yet, what I will paint, but I know it will be something soothing and peaceful." She sure hoped that's what he wanted to hear.

"I stayed for quite some time looking at the canvas but, not being exactly sure what I should paint, I left the canvas and turned my attention to the oils. Some of the tubes needed to be burped, so I carefully unrolled the ends of each tube and pushed the air out of them. I must not have done this procedure after my last painting—a definite error on my part, but one that I was able to correct before the paints began to dry."

"After that was completed, I went to the kitchen where I made myself a luncheon comprised of a turkey wrap, two dill pickles, and six carrot sticks, all placed on a paper towel which, once I had completed my meal, I threw into the garbage. I retired to my room and read for a while. By three o'clock, I was feeling rather fatigued, so I had a nap in the afternoon, but was awakened when I heard the front door open and close. I don't know who returned from where, but I got up, combed my hair and joined the other women in the common room. They were, of course, watching Oprah. Her show yesterday was about hip-slimming fashions and Delta Burke was her guest designer." Elizabeth chuckled and veered from her script. "That's humorous, because Delta Burke was on the TV show, *Designing Women*, but she didn't portray a designer on the show, she was actually the financial backer for her sister's business and really, all she ever did was bring clients to the firm, but now, here she is, in real life, a real life designer of clothes. Of course, her clothing is for larger women as she is a larger woman herself, but she did lose a great deal of weight several years ago, and I believe she has managed to keep it off." Swallow and breathe; return to the script.

"At five o'clock, Matron Evelyn came from the kitchen and informed everyone that supper was ready. I walked with my fellow house guests to the dining area where we supped on a delicious meal of spaghetti and meatballs created by…" she paused momentarily, not remembering what she had written as the woman's insignificant name. Improvising she continued, "That dear woman who is taking the cooking classes at the college." She added as an afterthought to Dr. Anderson, "She is doing remarkably well, you know. There was actually enough pasta for everyone last night, and although there was a little too much garlic on the garlic bread for my liking, it was quite palatable, as was the Caesar salad that she made."

Back to the script: "After supper, I returned again to the basement to try to muster inspiration for my canvas. I stared at it, gently rubbed my hands on it, and sat and stared at it again, but I was not yet able to determine what to paint, so I returned to my room where I read another chapter of the historical romance novel I got on our last trip to the library. I then prepared myself for bed, saw Matron Evelyn for my evening dose of medication, and returned to my bedroom where I recorded my notes, and, turning out the light, I eventually fell asleep."

That task completed, she smiled at Dr. Anderson as if to say, "There. Are you happy now?" She was hoping he would pick up on the whole I've-got-a-canvas-to-paint-and-I'm-trying-to-decide-what-to-paint-on-it-and-not-waiting-for-divine-inspiration-to-tell-me-what-to-paint blurb so she could discuss with him how dreadful the medication made her feel, but he honed in on the one part of her present experience that she hadn't yet fully rehearsed.

Black Blood

"Tell me about this morning's panic attack."

Shit. How did he know about that? She stared at him for a moment in amazement. Dr. Anderson did not look up from his notebook. He just waited, patiently, until she was ready to begin.

"I'm. Not. Sure. Why." She started slowly and mechanically, thinking of the events of today, "But I had. A panic. Attack. While I was washing. The dishes. This morning." Doctor Almighty remained silent, nodding his head, baiting her to go on, to express herself, to deal with her psychological intricacies on her own. When she resumed, she continued to pause after each phrase, but this time it was to accentuate her words for Doctor Almighty's entitlement, for his enjoyment, using the words she knew he wanted to hear. "But. I was able to overcome. The difficulty. With the deep breathing exercises. You taught me." From here, she wasn't sure how much of the attack to explain to him. She didn't know if she should tell him that she zoned out for about 20 minutes. She didn't know if she should expose the fact that she had felt extremely agitated by having her hands in the water, or that the sound of the water running into the sink made her feel nauseous, or that she had not completed the full realm of her duties because she just couldn't stand to be in the kitchen any longer. She didn't know if she had said enough to satisfy him that she had handled the panic attack all on her own, but when she saw the soft curl of his lips to indicate that he was pleased with what she had said, she stopped talking. She would just be quiet now—the ball was in his court.

Doctor Almighty allowed the pause to linger. When he lifted his head to speak to her, he led their conversation to Elizabeth's expectations of washing the breakfast dishes. He encouraged her to tell him the reasons why she had asked for this job. Elizabeth told him what he wanted to hear: she had asked for this job so she could work together with her housemates, to put to use her knowledge of socially acceptable interactions, and to prove that she could set a goal and work towards it.

She didn't dare tell him that the actual reason she had asked to wash the dishes was so she could start to self-medicate, and she had to stifle a grin as she thought about that. She spoke to him instead about remembering to address each woman by name when she brought to her their dirtied dishes. She reminded him, too, that under the guidance of Matron Janet, she had created the step-by-step guide for ensuring the morning tasks were broken down into manageable segments. She used it, she told him, as a measure of her success in completing the morning's ritual. It allowed her to focus on only one aspect of the job at hand, and to not become overwhelmed by the enormity of the concrete objects that physically surrounded her. She did not tell him, however, that during her panic attack this morning, she hadn't even remembered she'd made that stupid step-by-step plan, let alone use it.

Doctor Almighty seemed pleased with what she told him and steered their conversation to the responsibilities Elizabeth had taken on with this job. Responsibilities that could, he reminded her, cause conflict with her fears and phobias. First and foremost, he specified that the dishes could not be done if she was unable to put her hands into the water.

"Elizabeth, share with me some insight into what your body experienced this morning when you felt it necessary to remove your hands from the water."

Now, seriously. How could she respond to that? If he had said, "Can you explain what happened…" or "Would you like to share your thoughts…" she could say, "No." Done. End of conversation. Even if he asked the more direct, "Tell me what happened this morning…" she could answer, "Nothing." But this! For this query there was no quick, one word answer. She couldn't say, "Nothing." He already knew something had happened and he expected her to face the reality of being confronted by normal, everyday occurrences that would, or could, cause her anxiety level to increase.

And Elizabeth knew that he really wanted to know if the panic attack had been brought on by the black cells. But it hadn't been. Her heart lurched as her memory carried her back to earlier today, standing in the centre of the kitchen.

And what she remembered, what she had seen to cause her anxiety to escalate, were the looming, dirty, disgusting dishes covering every inch of the counter.

– 8 –

Never the Same

I am three. I don't know it yet, but this time when the men come in the ambulance to take my mommy to the hospital, she will not ever return. She will be sent from the emergency room to the psych ward, and eventually to the St. Thomas Psychiatric Hospital where she will remain until her self-inflicted death two years later.

My mother didn't pull a Susan Smith or an Andrea Yates. She didn't try to harm me or hurt me. She just forgot me. She stood in a corner of her bedroom and did not move for two days. She stood there, rock solid, while I begged her to answer me. I yanked on her nightie. I pulled on her arm. I kicked her in the leg. She did nothing except soil herself and drool. The lady next door heard me crying, screaming, and came over. She saw my mother's catatonic body and called the ambulance.

While we waited for the ambulance to come, the neighbour lady was very kind to me. She had helped me before when

Lorrie Werden

Mommy was sick, and often came to bring sandwiches or apples to me. She asked me now if I was hungry. I nodded. She picked me up and carried me to the kitchen. When she set me down on the floor, just inside the kitchen door, she took two steps back and her hands flew to her mouth. I heard her gasp and turned to look at her. Her eyes gaped as she scanned the countertop laden with dirty dishes and the mountains of caked on, rotting food. In disbelief, her eyes narrowed as she focused on the stove covered in filthy pots and pans, open boxes of corn flakes, cocoa powder, and baking soda. She allowed her hands to fall away from her face and with an inhaled breath of determination she swooped down to lift me up from the wreckage. She held me close to her as she tried to take in the mess, the filth, the smell.

She turned her attention to the table and the floor surrounding it. Every single liveable space was covered with my mother's papers. My mother spent her days sitting at the table with newspapers, magazines, flyers, and countless diaries, trying to create a better life, a perfect life. She cut and pasted into her diaries pictures of models whose shapes she would never be able to emulate. She snipped apart, then glued back together, pictures of designer homes in which she would never live. Articles about social events she could never attend were cut out, too, glued into her diary, then, using her Sharpie, she would draw a big, fat X across each of the articles' surfaces. Obituaries of hundreds of people she didn't know had been hacked out of the papers and Elmer glued into a diary, too. My mother's most extensive work came in the form of her

Black Blood

recording items from the weekly flyers. Deals of the century for bananas, shoes, refrigerators, chairs, snowmobiles, whatever, were placed in a book. Rather than being glued in, though, these cuttings were attached by scotch tape so that each Friday, when the new flyers arrived, she would cut out the newest, greatest deals, then move around the already acquired deals, in monetary order from least expensive to most expensive, so that she could fit the newly acquired bargains into the puzzle. This is what my mother did. This is how she found relief. This is how our life was.

The neighbour pushed a pile of diaries from the corner of the table towards the middle. She sat me on the exposed area of the table to free up her hands so she could remove newspapers from a chair. Once she had placed them on the floor, she plunked my butt onto the chair and turned to face the rest of the kitchen.

She made her way to the counter, swatting at fruit flies as she went. Lifting the dirty, dish-laden draining tray, she removed it from the counter and placed the whole filthy package on the floor near the stove to expose a small space on which she could work. She opened drawers until she found a clean-ish towel and, after wetting it, she washed the small space of newly uncovered Arborite. Just beyond this newly discovered treasure of cleanliness, she found a half loaf of bread hiding in the bread box. She asked me if I'd like a sandwich. The bread was only a little bit green so she tore off the mouldy bits from the crust. She found peanut butter in the cupboard above the stove and spread it on the bread with the long handle end of a tablespoon. Then she used the handle to cut the bread into triangles (I was very impressed with this trick) and, not being able to find a clean plate, put them on the corner of another towel she found in the drawer. Even though I was very hungry, I ate the pretty sandwiches very slowly, taking little nibbles off the corners of the triangles, biting at them until they formed the shape of a small circle. Once it was perfectly round and smooth, I popped the whole circle into my mouth and sucked it until the bread and peanut butter became one solid tablet in my mouth. It stuck to the roof of my mouth and I used my tongue to rub over it, back and forth, until it eroded and washed away with my spit.

The neighbour lady stood in front of the sink and asked if I wanted a drink. I looked up at her. Through the uncurtained window, the sun was shining all around her and she was enshrouded in a warm light. The sun caught the cut glass from her bauble necklace and splintered its rays into a thousand pieces all around her head. In that instant, the sun was so bright, that it caused a glow to pass over her face, totally eliminating her own facial features and replacing them with a multitude of heavenly colours. I knew right then that she was an angel that had been sent here to care for me, to look after me, to love me. It was the first time I believed in God. It was the first time I saw His beauty. It was the first time I felt the need to capture and hold onto the beauty of the yellows and golds, the blues and the greys, the vibrancy and electricity that I saw. With my eyes still affixed in amazement to her apparition, I nodded a confirmation for the drink. She moved away from the window and the bauble's captured light was immediately turned off. The room became dark again, and I felt a deep sadness that my commune with the heavens had been broken.

She looked in the fridge and pulled out glass bottles with liquid in them, but there was no milk or juice. She returned to the sink, pushed some dishes out of the way, and let the cold water run for a very long time. As she stood in front of the window, I searched her edges to find the celestial glow again, but it was gone. There were no bright colours emanating from her. In fact, a cloud had moved to cover the sun so that now there was no light coming in through the window at all. I realized that she wasn't an angel. She was just the neighbour lady, standing in my mommy's kitchen, running water into the sink.

She found a clean glass somewhere, filled it with water, and gave me a really cold drink of water. The liquid felt good as it washed the peanut butter off my tongue, off the roof of my mouth, and as it flowed into my belly when I swallowed. It tasted good, but it didn't make me feel as good as when I had seen the angel.

Just as I was finishing the sandwich, there was a knock at the door. I knew it was the men with the ambulance. Even though there were never, ever any sirens to announce their arrival, I knew it was them. The police were there, too, and they asked the neighbour if she could reach any relatives to look after me. The neighbour nodded. She had called my Nana before when my Mommy had been sick and she knew her phone number. As the attendants put Mommy's stiff body onto the stretcher, the neighbour and I left my house and crossed the yard to her front porch. While I sat on her swing, and watched the ambulance take my mother away, she went inside to call my Nana.

Two hours later, Nana came in a taxi to take me to her house. I never, ever went back to my own house. I never, ever saw the neighbour angel-lady again. I never, ever again ate a sandwich that had been cut into triangles, just for me.

I was never, ever the same again.

– 9 –

Two Week Plan

Elizabeth told him about the panic attack, and with the mention of each facet of the attack, Doctor Almighty's face warmed and comforted her. He never interrupted her, never had to ask her to continue. He just sat in his leather chair with his feet crossed up on his thighs, and watched her intently. Elizabeth envisioned an invisible bridge that spanned from her mouth to his belly, and watched as her words of the panic attack marched across that bridge to Dr. Anderson. When her words reached him, he accepted them, gathered them from her, and helped her to dispose of the burden of the attack. Periodically, he nodded his assent, and this compassion allowed the flow of words to continue from her, across the bridge, right to the safety of Doctor Almighty.

When she was finished explaining the occurrence, she felt spent, but in a comfortable, rested way. As she relaxed, Doctor Almighty commended her for persevering with her duties in the kitchen and for working through the panic attack. He was thrilled that she had used the deep breathing exercise to help calm herself. He was very pleased that she was taking an interest in the women around her and that she was able to give positive feedback about the meal created by Dora. (Oh, yeah, Elizabeth suddenly remembered. That's who made the spaghetti—Dora the Douche.) He also commended her for continuing to gain skills in handling different social interactions and he used her trips to the library and joining the women in the lounge as examples of when she had used these skills.

"I must say, Elizabeth," he warmed, "your recovery is going very well. I know you want to return to your apartment and I think, with your increasing ability to set goals and to stick to them, you are right on track to go home in two weeks. Well done."

He closed his notebook and gave her one more directive. Her homework was to devise, and implement over the next 14 days, an actual plan for her return to the apartment! Elizabeth heard this, but really could not believe her ears. She knew that her release from the halfway house was coming soon, but for some reason, the time frame of two weeks had not entered her cognizance as a meagre 14 days. Now, it did. Two weeks was not the greater part of a month's calendar page, it was only 14 single days, each day represented by only one tiny square on the calendar! Fourteen days in which she must create plans—plans toward going home. She was elated. She really, truly tried to listen to what Doctor Almighty was saying then, but her head was filled with exploding fireworks and she was enjoying the realization that came with each explosion. Home! Freedom! Painting!

In between bursts, she caught a few snippets of what the good doctor was saying, "…create a plan…Matron Evelyn return your paints…take the bus…take a taxi…record your needs…grocery list…Matron Joan…new medications… appropriate for your return." She didn't catch it all, but the phrases she did hear confirmed what the doctor had said: She was really, truly going home. Once she was finished her session with Doctor Almighty, she fled to her room, threw herself down onto the bed, pulled the pillow over her head, and cried with joy.

The two weeks absolutely flew by. Elizabeth had energy to spare the first week and she had every reason to be excited—she was going home! That first week, after Doctor Almighty had dangled his 'REHABILITATED' rubber stamp in front of her like a carrot, Elizabeth was consumed with creating, devising, editing, and revising her 'Return to My Apartment' plan. She and Dr. Anderson had met and discussed it, time and time again, until they were both comfortable with the plan. Ultimately, nothing could move forward until Doctor Almighty gave the plan his final approval, and that didn't come until the Friday of the first week.

"Excellent work, Elizabeth. You must be incredibly proud of yourself. Tell me which part of your plan is most important to you." Elizabeth knew that immediately. She was most excited to return to painting. She could not wait to be back in her own apartment, completely without medication, so her thoughts and musings could become reality on the canvases that waited for her. She didn't tell Doctor Almighty this, though. She answered simply, "Painting in my own apartment with the natural light from the windows." Doctor Almighty knew that the basement was not a reasonable place for her to paint, but she had been very grateful that he had allowed her any space at all. Yes, the women were allowed to bring their hobbies to the halfway house with them, such as stupid Rubik's cubes or word search books, but these hobbies took up very little space. Elizabeth's hobby took up a huge amount of space and the only place in the house that had enough room to accommodate her was the basement.

She had continued her duties as dishwasher, and had elected to ply her ruse on the Matrons on alternate days. She had finally learned how to expel all six of the pills and she felt by rejecting them all on alternate days, it still allowed her to keep a good portion of her brain free from the weight of the medications. She was enjoying the feelings of inspiration as they came into that part of her awakened brain, but the other part, the still frozen part of her brain, screamed for revival. She knew, though, that she couldn't release it from its prison until she returned to the safety of her own apartment.

She had painted quite a bit recently, but Elizabeth had felt very controlled and rigid in her painting style. She had completed two pictures, just small ones, only 18" by 24," but she liked them, even though she did not feel at the top of her creativity. She entitled one 'The Muse,' and the second was 'Country Lane. ' They were both as different as if two separate artists had painted them.

'The Muse,' painted in portrait view, was an icy, silvery, representation of a woman sitting on a rock near the ocean. In the painting, the woman's long, blonde hair blew away from her face as the wind whipped her frayed gown up and around, down and around, around and around her body, the rock, and out into the ocean. Fringes of the dress became blended with the wind and the waves, and looked as if, at any moment, the woman could be sucked into the sea, or blown away with the wind. For Elizabeth, it represented a meeting of two worlds: one pulling the woman towards reality; one pushing the woman away from it.

Her second painting, 'Country Lane,' started out as a simple landscape piece, but the more Elizabeth worked on it, the more the imagery became embedded in its reflections. In the foreground of the picture, the viewer saw mostly trees, ground cover, shrubbery, and flowers of the forest. But this painting had the unique ability to allow the viewer to see past the entrance of the forest and focus on a road that manifested itself once you looked past the trees. In typical artwork, a road begins broadly at the bottom of the canvas and travels away from the viewer. The width of the road becomes narrower as it snakes up the canvas, giving the illusion of fading off into the distance. 'Country Lane,' however, did the exact opposite. Looking at this picture, you could see the road expanding before you. It was as if a view of the whole forest had just opened up, showing the viewer millions and millions of wonderful things to explore. Elizabeth had hidden etchings of people's faces among the greenery and in the dust of the lane. It was a picture that one could look at for a very long time and still not see every profile hidden within. Her housemates loved it.

"Oh, is that me?"

"Look, it's Matron Evelyn."

"That's not her—she's over here."

In truth, Elizabeth had painted no one in particular; she had just combined different facial features to create the looks. The women liked most of the faces, but there were the others, the sinister and foreboding faces hidden deep within the dark parts of the trees' root systems, upon which they did not, could not, linger. These were cold and harsh—frightening. So they allowed their gazes to return to the faces that felt familiar and comfortable.

On Saturday, Elizabeth covered her four completed canvases and took a cab to Yvonne's art gallery, *Diva d'Art*.

"My God, Elizabeth! These are magnificent." Elizabeth hadn't seen Yvonne since she had gone into the hospital. Prior to her hospitalization, Elizabeth had been quite prolific and had brought numerous paintings to Yvonne. One humungous canvas, filled with visions and predictions, was so big that it had to be brought to the gallery in a moving van. Yvonne had kept the canvases safely tucked away in her climate controlled storage room until there were enough paintings for a second show.

Black Blood

Yvonne had been a longtime friend of Elizabeth's. Both she and Angela Westland, Social Worker, had been great supporters of Elizabeth's art. When Elizabeth turned 16, and was no longer eligible for a social worker through the Children's Aid Society, she and Nana had tried to make a go of it on their own. But after Elizabeth's first hospitalization, Angela had been assigned to her through the outpatient's department at St. Benedict's. Angela was with the Canadian Mental Health Association and had helped Elizabeth get through the rest of high school, through Nana's death, and the sale of her house. Working with a lawyer as the power of attorney, Angela had ensured that the proceeds from the sale had been set up, in trust, for Elizabeth. It was the lawyer, too, who had informed her of the cache of other money that had been left to Elizabeth. When Elizabeth was eight, Nana had been involved with lawyers and court things, but she had never discussed this with Elizabeth. Upon Nana's death, however, the lawyer informed her of the trust account that had been started with settlement money Nana had received after the wrongful death of Elizabeth's mother while she was a patient in the hospital. Elizabeth had no idea that there was any money. As far as she knew, they lived, for all those years, off of some kind of pension that Nana had. Elizabeth, too, when she came of age, got some government money, but it was not very much. But the settlement was; it was a lot of money. So much money, in fact, that Elizabeth (with assistance from Angela and Yvonne) had been able to purchase her loft apartment. Yvonne and the lawyer helped Elizabeth manage the money from the sales of her pictures, too. Yvonne had already held one proper showing and Elizabeth's works had been purchased both locally and internationally. She even had a painting purchased by, and shipped to, General Sheikh Mohamed bin Zayed Al Nahyan, the Crown Prince of Abu Dhabi. Being one of the largest canvases Elizabeth had ever painted, 'The Storm' was in the private study of the Sheikh, adorning the greater part of the wall behind his writing table. Elizabeth's commission from this transaction had solidified her financial stability.

In the second set of seven short days before her return home, there were a million little tasks that had to be done. On Monday, she had to return the library book. She hadn't quite finished it yet, so she stayed up very late on Sunday night to read it to the very end. That night, she dreamed of the maiden, lost at sea, who was never again to see her lover. When she slept, Elizabeth saw him, the lover, in her dreams. He was very tall, much taller than she. In the confines of her dream, Elizabeth became the maiden. She was close to the lover. Her hands, placed on his naked chest, were able to feel the heat from his skin against her. She could feel the lover's arm go behind her back and pull her body towards him. Her arms went up to reach around his neck. He had long hair and she wrapped her fingers through it. She looked intently at his face, but couldn't really make out his features. She just saw strength and masculinity, desire and wanting. She wanted him, too. He leaned forward and placed his lips on hers. She could taste the saltiness of his saliva as

Black Blood

his tongue pushed its way between her lips and into her mouth. Elizabeth felt his heat rush into her and she pulled him closer to her, revelling in the nearness of him, revelling in his strength. She could feel herself grinding against him, feeling the heat of her own body climbing to reach his. But then, she awoke, and the dream was done. She felt mildly embarrassed by the eroticism of her dream, but Elizabeth wished the dream had continued until she had made love to the unknown man. When she returned the book to the library on Monday, she placed it gently in the 'Return' bin and rubbed the cover lovingly, as if saying goodbye to a very dear friend.

On Tuesday, Elizabeth had to go to the pharmacy to have her newest prescriptions from Doctor Almighty filled. When she entered the pharmacy located near her apartment, the young woman behind the check-out counter glared at her for a moment. Elizabeth could see that she was taking an immediate inventory of Elizabeth's appearance. Hair brushed. Eyes calm. Clothes neat. Elizabeth could read the woman's face as clearly as if she were screaming out, "The crazy lady is here, but it's OK. She's not freaked out." Elizabeth made her way back to the pharmacist, the prescription held tightly in her hand. Doctor Almighty could have called the prescription into the apothecary, but it was important to him that Elizabeth be responsible for getting the medication; as if going through the process of riding the bus, walking for two minutes from bus stop to store front, presenting her 'get out of jail free' card to the pharmacist, and returning to the halfway house, bag in hand, was a series of actions proving to him that she was committed to being well and would continue to take the medications. Hah!

On Wednesday, Elizabeth carefully packed up her paints. She washed each brush with turpentine, carefully formed the cleansed bristles into the expected, pristine-new shapes, and slid them gently between the plastic grips that held them in place in the canister. The cap on each tube of paint was twisted to the right to ensure the tubes were well sealed, and Elizabeth placed them in their carrying case ensuring she matched them to the correct colour-coded site. She wiped down all the bottles of paint thinner and turpentine, turning their lids, too, to ensure they would not leak. The empty, begging-to-be-painted-on canvases were lovingly placed in their wooden box, and then, using a small palette knife, Elizabeth gently scraped off bits of dried paint from her easel before folding it up and carrying everything upstairs. Matron Evelyn went with her on the bus to help lug everything back into her apartment. Matron Evelyn was actually quite helpful that day. She was a big, strong woman, who easily carried the easel and the box of canvases. Elizabeth carried her beloved paints and the small crate that housed the liquid cleaners and the canister of brushes.

Elizabeth also carried with her all the new medications. Once into her loft apartment, and with her painting gear settled in the work area, she and Matron climbed the stairs to the bathroom. There, she handed the (nearly full) bottles of old medications to Matron Evelyn, and replaced them with the new, pretty bottles of medicine, knowing that they, too, would remain here, unopened, for a long, long time.

On Thursday, Elizabeth had to ensure she had all her own clothes. This wasn't too difficult a task for her; she did not share her clothing with any of the other women. They liked to do that, share their clothes, and Elizabeth guessed it was a way to socially interact with her housemates, but she just didn't want to be part of that barter and trade system.

"Can I borrow your blue shirt? You can wear my new jeans."

"Did you take my jacket, bitch? It is *not* in the closet."

"What happened to my fucking shoes? Who the hell wore my shoes? You broke the goddamned heel."

Since Elizabeth did not join in this game of clothing camaraderie, she did not have to worry about missing or ruined apparel. She had only to ensure that all of her clothes were washed, dried, and folded, and ready to travel home. She kept a change of clothes in an overnight bag along with her comb, toothbrush and toothpaste, deodorant, and one extra pair of underwear.

Friday, she took the bus from the halfway house to the grocery store. Part of her 'Return to My Apartment' plan was to ensure that she had enough food in stock. Last week, she made a grocery list and went over it with Doctor Almighty. She had already been working with Matron Joan on devising nutritious meal plans so she was able to create her grocery list by following the different menus. Elizabeth's usual grocery shopping habits were sporadic at best, particularly when she was off her medication. When she was elevating, she had a tendency to buy too much fresh produce that would become rotten long before she had the chance to eat it. When she was spiralling, she would have no fresh foods at all, and she subsisted on dry corn flakes, Sun Chips, and Sunny-D. The nutritionist, Matron Joan, ensured that Elizabeth learned Canada's Food Guide. She learned that she must "eat a wide variety of different foods from each food group every day" and her grocery list had to reflect this knowledge. She learned what portion sizes were and this, too, was reflected in the grocery list. If she was going to have one cup of salad at each of her seven supper meals for the week, she did not need to purchase seven heads of lettuce. She proudly showed Doctor Almighty that she was going to purchase only one head of leaf lettuce, and only one head of romaine, for the week.

Her grocery bags in tow, Elizabeth caught another bus to take her home. She suspected that perhaps one of the Rotund Ugly Matrons would already be at her apartment waiting for her to show up, but as she walked, she noted the sidewalk outside her building was empty. Doctor Almighty had told her she could have the companionship of one of the Matrons to go shopping with her if she wanted, but she really wanted to do this on her own. He commended her for showing this example of determination in completing her own goals. The only thing he required was that she return to the halfway house before supper, then meet with Matron Joan to review the grocery store receipt to ensure her purchases matched all the necessary items on her list.

Black Blood

And then it was Saturday! Oh, sweet, wonderful, day of freedom. Elizabeth was excited beyond belief, but for the most part, she was able to contain herself. There was only one incident at lunch that had flustered her. When the Lesbian from London and the Cunt from Caledonia got into an argument over which mug of coffee belonged to which woman, Elizabeth had been able to feel the tension between the two of them. Their voices were strained, and although they did not raise them, to Elizabeth's ears their squabbling became louder and louder. The force with which their voices penetrated her brain was crushing. The squabbling spread so rapidly and forcefully into her head that Elizabeth jumped up from her place at the table to back away from their noise. When she stood, her chair went flying, and the sudden bang with which it hit the floor interrupted the argument. Everyone's head snapped toward Elizabeth and the room went dead silent. The terror-struck looks on their faces as they glared at her struck Elizabeth as horrifically funny, and her agitation immediately turned to abandoned laughter. She snickered. She guffawed. And the women slowly turned their heads away but kept their eyes on her, watching, as she backed herself up against the wall and continued to laugh.

Elizabeth didn't want them looking at her anymore and even though she was still laughing, their staring eyes penetrated through her opened mouth. She clutched her hands together, one over the other, and placed them over her mouth. This stopped their stares from infiltrating into her body and they soon went back to their own undertakings.

Elizabeth, though, remained at the wall. Snickers seeped from her lips but she couldn't remember why she was laughing. She wanted to stop, but something was so funny that it continued to tickle her right from the inside.

The women finished their lunches, and even though it was Saturday and they had nowhere else to be, they quickly washed their dishes and departed from the kitchen. Elizabeth was left alone, still standing against the wall and tittering into her hand, when Matron Beatrice came to address her behaviour. Matron stood right in front of Elizabeth, uncomfortably close, and looked deep into her eyes. "Elizabeth!" Matron bellowed. Elizabeth hiccupped and inhaled a few small, quick breaths, but then a longer, refreshing inhale of breath that quieted her laughter.

She knew immediately that Matron Beatrice was scanning her to fit her into the one-to-ten crazy list, but Elizabeth played the move first. "Oh, Matron," she gushed. "Please, excuse me." Elizabeth placed her hands on Matron's forearms for accentuation. "I am just so overwhelmed that I get to go home today, and one of the girls said something funny, and we laughed, but then I started to think about how I would be going home today, and it just gave me such delight that I became giddy." She wanted to say more but she knew when to shut her mouth. She returned Matron's stare, then inhaled audibly so that Matron would know she was gaining control of herself. She exhaled with the same intensity, and inhaled again. Matron Beatrice took a step back so Elizabeth's hands were no longer touching her, but as she backed away, Elizabeth realized she had been holding onto Matron just a little too tightly. She quickly clasped her hands in front of her chest and lowered her gaze from Matron's face. She allowed a silence to grow so Matron could see that she was now calm.

After a few moments, Elizabeth raised her head and looked at Matron Beatrice. Matron's eyes had gone from the strained observation of judging a crazy scale, to soft pools of chocolate brown. They weren't her Nana's eyes, but something in them reminded Elizabeth of the time when her Nana had touched her cheek and Elizabeth felt warm and soothed. The craziest urge came over her, and she had no idea why she did it, but she gently took the one step forward to Matron Beatrice, and she hugged her. "Thank you," she said to Matron, "for all your help these past few weeks, and please extend to the other Matrons as well my sincere gratitude for helping me through this rough period." Oh, it was syrupy and sappy and the words felt foreign to her as they spewed out of her mouth, but somehow, she really meant them. She dropped her arms back down to her side and retreated the one step.

Matron's face softened and the 'REHABILITATED' smile formed on her lips. Elizabeth saw it and she could actually feel its warmth spread throughout her body. The token smile somehow spoke volumes to Elizabeth and provided her with an overwhelming feeling of comfort. The feeling was so unexpected that tears actually welled up in Elizabeth's eyes. She looked away, embarrassed by this show of emotion.

Matron took Elizabeth's hand in her own and gave it a gentle squeeze, but the tender moment was broken when the A-hole from Aylmer yelled, "Your taxi's here." Matron turned and walked toward the front door. Elizabeth followed her, grabbed her jacket from the hook in the hallway and picked her overnight bag up from off the floor.

Without a word to anyone, Elizabeth walked over the threshold of the halfway house, down the porch steps, and got into the taxi. She was almost home.

– 10 –

Inner Attack

It is Friday, the 29th day of February, 2008. It is a leap year. A year with an extra day. A day with a date that will not occur again until 2012, so that in 2009 I won't have to say, "Oh, my God. It's February the 29th. It's been a full year since my last show. What have I done since then?"

It is the opening night of my very first exhibition at Diva d'Art Gallery *and I am seated on my own little chair just outside of Yvonne's office, away from everyone else. Yvonne runs to me, flooding me with her presence before I even have time to think about exiting from my self-imposed isle of solitude. She positively gushes at me, "Oh, Elizabeth. The show is going so well!"*

As I rise up from the chair, I struggle to push her out of the way so I can actually stand. She grabs my hands into hers and squeezes them as she tells me, "I've sold two more—'The Eclipse' and 'Unwanted'. They've both sold!" In her excitement,

Lorrie Werden

her nails dig into my palms and it hurts. I stiffen. She understands immediately. She drops my hands, and takes a quick step back. She realizes she has broken into my inner circle, and in a split second her facial expressions go from glee, to regret, to sympathy, but I can see the changes as clearly as if they had been performed in slow motion. She retreats yet another step and clasps her hands in front of her chest, a token symbol that she will not touch me again. "You need a drink," she oozes. "I'll be right back." She turns and disappears into the crowd while I rotate back to my isle that is the armchair by her office door. She doesn't come back with a drink because she knows I am not yet of legal drinking age. She also does not return because she knows she must not talk to me now until the show is over. She knows I have a metered quotient of acceptable social behaviour and it must all be used on the patrons. She will not waste any more of that precious proportion with her drivel.

Alone again, I melt into the chair, fold my hands on my lap, and although I turn my head away from them, I can feel the eyes of the groups of people upon me. I have to be here. Yvonne said so. She said I have to be in attendance so the people can see me, can meet me. She has reviewed with me all the social graces I must endure, but I hate it. I hate the people. There are too many people here, all standing around, staring at me, gawking at my work. The worst ones are the people who have already purchased my art. They want to touch me, to shake my magical hands, and to thank me for the paintings that grace their homes. They need to tell me that they are the envy of all their friends now that they are the proud owners of a work by the oh-so-young, prolific, painting genius, Elizabeth Devereux. Through clenched teeth, I will smile, let them fondle me, touch me, then escape from their grasp with the practised, and socially acceptable, "I'm glad you are enjoying that painting. Please excuse me. I must mingle." Then, with my head down, I will shuffle between a few clusters of people before returning to my corner to slink back into this chair. I will wait for the next swarm of buzzing idiots to advance upon me, but when I see them looming, I will rise quickly from my seat and move toward them for I do not want their presence to break the invisible barrier around my chair that I have created to keep these monsters at bay. I want to keep them away from my private corner, away from my small isle of isolation.

I am suddenly surreally aware of the great hoard of people stuffed into this building. Sitting on my throne, I can see them milling around my paintings. They turn to me, nudging their companion with a "there she is, the painting protégée" elbow, and a finger point. I hate being here and they know it, but they come toward me anyway and, like a knight defending his castle, I must protect this corner. Each time I advance toward the enemy, each time I guard my sanctuary from their intrusion, each time I go undercover into the mingling crowd, and each time I covertly retreat to my isle of isolation, it uses a fraction of my socially acceptable congeniality. For an eternity I endure this insufferable ritual then retreat, self-presentation into self-preservation.

Lorrie Werden

By eleven o'clock, the crowd has thinned, but the ones who remain are the really needy ones. They are the ones who wait until everyone else has gone so they can catch me alone to share some kind of spiritual interaction with me. They need to speak to me. They need to touch this young, slip of a girl who has so much potential. They need to love me. They need to become my friend. They need to fix me. They are no longer interested in my art, they are now only interested in me and, like a pack of wolves surrounding a frightened lamb, they come toward me, advancing for one final attack into my isle of sanctuary. I am dangerously close to the end of my social compliance levy. I do not have enough resources to deal with this throng of people. My palms are sweaty, my vision becomes blurred, and the once tranquil music with its running water and chirping birds now grates in my eardrums like a train's rusty brakes. As I look at them stalking me, my breathing becomes more rapid and my heart begins to race. I need to leave.

I stand up and thrust myself backwards towards Yvonne's office. My outstretched hand reaches to grab the doorknob, but I know I cannot turn it. I cannot go in to her office without her permission. That would make me one of them, one of the interlopers, one of the invaders, one of the hated. I will not break this trust with her. I quickly scan the crowds to try to find her to obtain her permission, but I can't see her. My throat is closing, gripped so tightly with anxiety that I can't even yell her name. My legs are cement and I can't leave this position. I am frozen on this spot and I close my eyes to shut

Black Blood

out the crowd. Closing myself off from them, I retreat into a black abyss. My body becomes a stone wall of defence and I am removed from this place, from these people, from my art, and from my fear. I am safely consumed by darkness.

Much later, when I am able to hear Yvonne's voice speaking to me, I allow myself to focus on her words. "They are gone now," she whispers. "See? I've turned off the lights and the music. There are no more people here—just you and me. We'll just wait here, OK? Until you are ready to go. We'll just wait."

I hear her before I can see her. When it registers with my brain that the atmosphere is calm and quiet, I'm able to focus on the gallery around me. It is quiet. Dead quiet. I breathe in the stillness and manage to open my eyes. The only things left of my show are a clutter of glasses on a tray near the front door, and used napkins strewn on the floor. Yvonne has turned off the bright, overhead spotlights leaving only the softly lit pot lights to illuminate the area. She has brought a chair close to me, but has kept it away from my sanctioned circle. She's sitting forward on it, forearms resting on her thighs, slouching over a glass of wine that she is rocking back and forth between her thumb and forefinger. She is not looking at me, but she continues to talk to me, nonsensical stuff, in a hushed voice. "We're all alone now. The crazy people are gone. No more hands to shake. No more questions to answer. No more intruders. You're safe now. It's just you and me. All alone. No other people." She sighs and moves to take a drink from her glass.

Lorrie Werden

When she sits up and tips her head back to receive the liquid libation, she notices that I am looking at her. She lowers her glass and smiles at me. "Welcome back," she says in the same quiet voice. "You OK?" I am able to nod my head in confirmation.

"Would you like to sit down now?" she asks, and tips her glass forward as a gesture towards my chair. I blink and swallow the saliva that has gathered under my tongue. I move my jaw, and elongate my neck to release the tension that has gathered there and in my shoulders. Slowly, my body is coming back to life. I make a miniscule turn with my head to look at my chair and slowly reach my hand toward it. My feet shuffle to move me toward the chair and automatically my knees bend as I sit.

"Would you like a drink of water?" she questions. I am able to move my head back and forth just enough so that she can recognize the motion as a "No, thank you." She knows I just need to sit for a moment. I suddenly realize I have to pee so badly that the backlog is making my bladder hurt, but I don't yet have the presence of mind to commit to making a movement that big. It will be a few minutes before my body catches up to my head. I am able to control my parasympathetic nervous system enough that I've swallowed my spit and I haven't yet pissed myself, but the messages to my arms and legs are not yet being received as quickly as they should be. I need to sit. I need to breathe. I need to emerge from myself.

For twenty full minutes, I continue to breathe. I allow the quiet to penetrate throughout my body as I inhale through

Black Blood

my nose. Yvonne has stopped talking. She is sitting back in her chair, her legs crossed, and she is enjoying her drink. She, too, is looking around the gallery. I follow her gaze to see that she is looking at all the sold signs displayed on my art. Out of twenty paintings, only three do not display this badge of honour—one large canvas and two smaller ones. Yvonne will have to put the big one back into storage, but she'll probably keep the smaller ones in the gallery. I know she has a show by another artist coming soon, but she'll have time to sell these little ones before that day.

I exhale long and slow. I'm glad the show went well. I don't care that the paintings sold, but I know it's important to Yvonne. She'll make a good commission off this sale and she's pleased. I can see it in her face. She has a far away, dreamy look, like she's already spending the money. I smile, too.

It is good. I relax. The tension leaves my body and I become connected again to my limbs. My muscles relax and my toes move inside my shoes. I inhale a deep, cleansing breath, and I am at peace.

– 11 –

At the End of Wellington Street

Elizabeth settled herself smack-dab in the middle of the backseat as she got ready to enjoy the luxury of travelling home in the taxi. She gave the driver her address and sat with ardent anticipation as he manoeuvred the car north toward the business section of Richmond Street. She purposefully sat in the middle of the car so she could see equally well out the back seat windows and still have a clear view through the front glass. Her eyes jumped with excitement as they scanned in panoramic vision: left-side, right-side, front, and driver; left-side, right-side, front, and driver. She looked with intent as the cab passed business after business, taking her toward the corners of Wellington Street and Central Avenue. No matter where she was in the city, whether she was riding or walking, reaching those corners denoted her envisioned mark of being halfway home.

Lorrie Werden

At Central Avenue, after the beauty of Victoria Park, square cinder block buildings of the business section magically gave way to a concoction of century old, beloved brick houses. The commercial landscape of concrete lawns and asphalt yards gave way to emerald green grass, fragrant flowering bushes, and well-used welcome mats. Making the transition from south of Central to north of Central along Wellington was always exciting for Elizabeth. It was like leaving behind the yellow brick road and finally passing through the gates leading to the Land of Oz. Great towering oak trees bent their branches to create a welcoming canopy for her return. The canopy spread for the full four blocks from Central to Pall Mall Street but stopped immediately at the corner of Pall Mall. Elizabeth knew why the canopy ended. It was so nothing would block the view of the majestic building standing directly in front of them at the dead-end of Wellington Street.

In a previous life, the big grey building had proudly housed up 175 workers. In the late 1800's, those workers made induction coils for some of the first telephones. The mid 1900's brought platinum electrodes, then uninsulated telephone wires, then vacuum tubes for black and white console televisions. And, by the 1970's, solid-state electronics had replaced those tubes. For many years after, other companies tried their hands at producing successful enterprises in the building, but the speed with which modern technology rendered their products obsolete was staggering. The old building still had good bones, but its internal workings were not able to keep up with the demands to produce modern technology.

The nail that finally sealed the casket of these struggling businesses occurred when CN Rail cut the track of transportation right out from under them. Pedestrians and motorists were wasting precious time when waiting for trains to cross over their passageway. The complaining travellers did not see the beauty in the back and forth waltz of shunting cars and switching tracks—they saw only the minutes ticking away as the red lights flashed a warning that they must not pass through, or go around, the outstretched arms of the sentinel. The city struck a deal with CN to re-route these trains further south and the community celebrated the removal of the busy trains by creating small, communal green spaces on either side of the street. They did not care that the cost of their few moments of gained time was the trouncing of countless jobs and possible business opportunities. They knew only that their own agendas, in both flight and fancy, would be kept on time.

With its era of trade gone, the big grey building sat empty for several decades. At the eleventh hour, just as the four-storey structure was to surrender to the city's chopping block, a Toronto developer swooped in and saved it from demise. Re-zoned from commercial usage to residential, the developers purchased the edifice for an amount that kept the city happy and ultimately paid for the upkeep of the green spaces. The renovations took months, with no expense spared to turn it into a statuesque showcase of downtown living.

Two bottom floors became 16 apartments that occupied the space where there once had been conveyer belts, loading zones, and offices. On upper levels, four two-storey condominiums took full-height advantage of both the third and fourth floors. The two condos on the south side boasted a magnificent living space that occupied the main floor, but it was the second level of these that was the true masterpiece. After ascending the spiral staircase, the floor opened to reveal master suites that rivalled the beauty and elegance of any European five-star hotel. Bathroom floors made of marble, gleaming bedroom walls of mahogany with chiselled inlays of ebony, and towering ceilings adorned with reclaimed, highly polished copper, created the picture frame for a masterpiece of grandeur living contained within. Natural gas fireplaces, gargantuan walk-in closets, a sunken hot tub, and two built-in, wall-mounted water features created an existential oasis of luxury and extravagance.

Of these two purchased abodes, only one had a full-time resident. Elizabeth had never met the secret owner of this condominium. She had, however, had the honour of meeting several guests who had stayed in the other condo. That beautiful residence had been purchased by the University of Western Ontario as a guest suite. Visiting professors, laureates, authors, lecturers, and no less than three Nobel Prize winners had graced this building. Some came with their families and stayed a semester. Some came overnight, just as a layover between speaking engagements. No matter how long they stayed though, the bevy of brains and creators that came and went from between these walls always left behind small pieces of their brilliance that searched out, and found, their way to Elizabeth. She loved it when new people stayed at the building. She could feel their energy, their intelligence, and their life force. She could feel it now as she entered the grand foyer. She had been gone for a long time and bits of discarded cogency and power of the great minds who had visited during her absence permeated her skin, awakened all her senses, and welcomed her home. Even though she had popped in over the past week to prepare for her homecoming, she hadn't taken the time to absorb the fact that she was home. She saved that moment for right now when she knew she would be staying.

She punched in her code and took the central elevator up to the third level. Once the lift had nestled into its stopped position, Elizabeth exited and veered right, to the door that marked entry into her sanctuary. She had her keys at the ready and slipped quickly into the vestibule of her loft. As often happened to her when she walked into her piece of heaven, Elizabeth was immediately overcome with the beauty of natural light that emitted into her space. The two side-by-side condos that occupied the back of the building had had the ceiling above the living areas completely eliminated, allowing the edifice to have magnificent 20-foot ceilings. Like its abutting neighbour, Elizabeth's residence had eight massively wide, northern exposure windows that ran a full 16 feet in height, centered between the floor and the ceiling. The array of windows in Elizabeth's abode continued around the eastern side of the building so that the earliest of sunrays could peek into her space and illuminate her world. Although a small but comfortable living quarter was configured along the south wall of the condo, the rest of the loft was a working space in which an artist could flourish.

When Elizabeth was in that creative space set far away from hypomania, but not yet into hypermania, those glimpses of the rising eastern sun lightened the nook where she liked to work on her smaller pictures. Her favourite easel (the one from Nana) always sat in this corner, turned at an angle so it could capture the natural light. The light would spread across the canvas allowing Elizabeth to see the flood of diverse colours that would soon become a solid piece of art. Once she got the initial image onto the canvas, she turned the easel around so the sun then shone directly in her eyes, continuing to burn the image onto her retinas as she transferred that imagery onto the canvas. When she was ready to do the more intricate, finishing work, she moved the easel clockwise so her shadow blocked out the continued flashing of the sun's rays. Now the creativity came from her impassioned heart. With careful concern, Elizabeth lovingly added the unique, hidden images that captivated her works' audiences. Sometimes, Elizabeth became so connected to the images she was painting, so in tune with the emotion she needed to portray, that her sensations were visible and audible. She would laugh and giggle, weep and mourn. Her enraptured body displayed the joy and happiness, as well as the loneliness and grief her pictures were meant to display. She loved to feel these strong emotions, to relish in the sensations that wracked her body. When she was finished painting a truly inspired picture, she felt exhausted, mentally and physically, often sleeping for days before she regained enough energy to resume her life.

Ensuring the door was locked behind her, Elizabeth now walked to the windows that bordered her view of the world, and stood with her arms wrapped around her waist. She closed her eyes and allowed the flow of the city to enshroud her. Taking a mental walk through her neighbourhood, she was able to absorb the life that she knew was out there. Although the majesty of Theatre London was invisible from her sight, she could feel her breath quicken as she sensed the nervous energy emanating from the actors waiting to take their place on the stage for the afternoon matinee. From farther south, the inaudible performances of previous musical arrangements from the likes of Moody Blues and Orchestra London slowed the rhythm of her heartbeat as she envisioned the musical notes leaping from the conductor's sheet music and dancing the six blocks from Centennial Hall to her loft. As she saw, through her mind's eye, the notes dancing through the landscape, they joined up with the music from bugles and tin penny whistles that had heralded ritualistic ceremonies and historical medieval festivals held at nearby Victoria Park. From across the park at Richmond Street, she sensed a bevy of colours from imported clothing and expensive bric-a-brac seep through the windows of the trendy shops along Richmond Row to join the parade of visual illusions that all sought a space in Elizabeth's mind. She allowed them to swirl there, enjoying their brilliance, before cataloguing them into various sensory sections of her brain.

She opened her eyes then, and looked farther north on Richmond Street. Melancholy swept past her as she caught a glimpse of the Stevenson-Lawson steeple, towering over the University of Western Ontario. She would not dwell on that feeling now; she would not let that memory cloud this day. She looked instead to where over 20,000 students made up the small city within the city, and watched as they spewed out from the gates of Western onto Richmond. The movements of the undergrads made up the rippling multi-cultural blanket that covered the strip below her. Every nationality, every creed, and every country was represented by students converging at the corners of Richmond and Oxford. She loved seeing the people together, students her age just being young and carefree, interacting with long time London residents. She watched the university girls tittering together, heads close as they shared a secret. She watched the elderly women juggle their yellow No Frills bags while attempting to manoeuvre their walkers around the group of Rastafarians gathered in front of the Bank of Montreal.

Over the course of a semester, Elizabeth had also watched as young love blossomed between newly connected couples. She could tell when a couple first hooked up. They walked side by side, shoulders close, but not quite touching. They were allowing their new partner into their own personal space, but not so close as to feel fully invaded. Soon, they would begin walking hand in hand, their need for personal space receding as quieter, more intimate conversations brought about the need to be in closer proximity to that person. When they began walking with their arms wrapped around each other's waists, their torsos so close together that they could be conjoined twins, Elizabeth knew they had surrendered their bodies to one another. They had invaded each other's personal spaces so deeply that the ancient, physical act of copulation had delivered them as one body, one soul, one mind. Whether or not they continued their relationship after their schooling was completed, Elizabeth had no idea. But for now, they were getting what they needed. They were getting the companionship of a peer, the sexual release from their horny, post-teenage thoughts, and the freedom to break as many rules as their family had fervently instilled in them.

When she did go out, Elizabeth never strayed very far from her neighbourhood. She took the bus sometimes to see Yvonne at the gallery in Byron, but she was most comfortable accessing the amenities that were within walking distance. She felt at home in this neighbourhood, safe. Alone, yet accompanied. When she was fluid and free of the drugs, she blended in with the life on these streets. Her sometimes unexpected verbal outbursts were commonplace here, just as commonplace as the outbursts from university students who had paid for, and ingested, hallucinogens to reach their own idea of nirvana. It was a sad irony that she had merely to relinquish her OHIP redeemed medications to feel the same inspired energy.

When the days of mania gave way to days of lowered functioning, she was no different than the homeless people who rooted themselves to a square of sidewalk just outside Mac's Milk on Oxford Street. Claiming a concrete quadrant as her own, usually in front of the familiar Shopper's Drug Mart, she would stand in comfort, just shrinking into herself as the rest of the world passed her by. Surprisingly, at dusk, her body knew enough to walk the three long blocks home to be safe from the creatures that came out in the depths of the night. She had heard about terrible things that had happened to the young women who stayed out on the streets and she did not want to become a statistic of rape. Nana had told her that men could do despicable acts to women, but Elizabeth's own sexual experiences with Corey (and yes, even with Trevor) had been wonderful and she did not want those memories marred by the savagery of some ruthless sex fiend.

She hugged herself as she thought of Corey. It seemed a lifetime ago, but the ease with which she could invoke her relationship with him was as real as if she were still mourning his departure. She didn't want to feel that loss now. She didn't want to relive the angst of being different and of having the only other person in the world that she thought knew her, and understood her, leaving, because he just could not deal with those differences.

Black Blood

The sun was setting now and Elizabeth watched as deep shadows formed along the sidewalks and benches that lined the backyard below her apartment. She had been standing here a long time and realized that her legs and shoulders were stiff. She stretched as she walked back through the working portion of her loft toward the living quarters. She looked toward the kitchen area wondering if she should eat some of the food she had purchased. She hadn't eaten anything since lunch, but she really was not hungry, and the kitchen, whose windows were blocked by large, built-in storage cabinets, seemed dark and uninviting. Elizabeth felt that if she entered there, her peace would be interrupted by its darkness. She wanted only to walk up the 20 steps to the open concept bedroom, take her night meds, crawl into bed, and let the warmth of being home spread under her, over her, around her, and through her, until she could feel its cocoon enfold her. Tomorrow, she would awaken a new butterfly ready for a dizzying flight of fancy.

– 12 –

Western Rodeo

I am nineteen and I have just royally fucked up my first year of post-secondary education.

Last year, in Grade 12, I worked my ass off to get a National Scholarship and to get accepted into the Visual Arts Program at the University of Western Ontario. For that full year, I studied and memorized shit that I knew I would never, ever, use again in my lifetime, but I needed nearly perfect marks to get into the program, and for the scholarship, so I just memorized everything and puked it all back up for exams so that my marks were way more than good enough to get in.

Memorizing the stuff was easy, but some of the other shit I had to do to get the scholarship wasn't so easy for me. Like, I had to hook-up with other people and play nicey-nice with them to get what I needed. Sorry: I had to practice my "people skills" (Dr. Anderson's words—NOT mine.) I had to ask the principal to fill out an Official Nomination Form for me and that had to be supported by Letters of Recommendation written by Very Important People, so that meant I had to grovel and make myself all Miss Goody-Two-Shoes to ask them to do it for me.

I talked to Yvonne and she had no trouble at all to write one. Her letter was actually pretty good, too. She said I was a "growing star with an intrinsic, prolific gift." She told them other crap, too, like how she'd already sold some of my stuff and that there was a "guaranteed market" for my "innovative creations," so that was good.

I got the art teacher to write one, too. I kinda liked Mrs. Brownlee, but she could be a bitch sometimes, so I had to be extra nice to her for a while. I must have caught her on a good day when I asked her to do the letter for me 'cause she told them in the letter that I was the "most gifted student" she had ever had the "privilege of teaching" and that my "extraordinary talent" was "beyond the scope" of her ability to teach me. Whatever.

I wasn't sure about asking Angela to write one. I didn't know if the university wanted to know that I was fruit-loops and had to have a social worker, but we got it all figured out 'cause Mrs. Margalis, the Resource Teacher, had to contact the Student Services Department at Western to transfer my whatever to them, so they did some kind of joint letter introducing me and, I guess, they told them that I needed a little extra TLC to cope with life, so that worked out.

The worst part about getting everything I needed for the scholarship was that I had to show "exceptional achievement in extracurricular activities." I had no idea what they wanted for that. Extracurricular activities to me meant like joining some kind of sports team and there was no fucking way I was going to try out for Track & Field! Mrs. Margalis rescued my ass for that one, too, though. She got me hooked up with the Drama Department and I painted backdrops for two of their plays. It was totally awesome actually—I was part of the club, but I didn't have to hang around any of the loser actors. It was bonus points too, 'cause I got to do it during school time so I didn't have to sit through Mr. Watson's Beyond Boring History class or Ms. DeMarco's Gimme A Break Geometry class.

I got to paint a huge mural on the chapel wall, too, and that was more bonus points for me because it fulfilled the Scholarship's requirement of "community service" and I got more time out of class, too, to do it.

But, if doing those two stupid things wasn't enough, I also had to do volunteer work. Mrs. Margalis got me a position at the London Library, copying pages and pages of old editions of Canadian Art *and* The Artist's Magazine *onto microfiche. It was my job to archive those magazines, but there was a definite upside to doing that 'cause all the tips and techniques they wrote about became engraved on my soul. It took me forever to get the magazines onto microfiche because I had to read and devour every single article before I could start copying them, but the techniques that I learned from the magazines helped me paint the stuff that eventually got me into the university's program, so that was good.*

Lorrie Werden

The bitch at the library once asked me why it was taking so long to get them done. I was not in a particularly good mood that day so I just yelled at her, "These are fuckin' volunteer hours—what do you care?" That was at the end of April. I think she couldn't wait to see the end of June—or the end of me.

Overall, that year sucked! My life was so fucking controlled. I had to be a good student. I had to be a good person. I had to be a good artist. I had to be a good patient. I had to be a good girl. I had to take my meds. I just had to be so fucking good that I couldn't do anything I really wanted to do. I had, like, these insurmountable, phenomenal ideas for paintings, but I couldn't do them the way I wanted to. I had this stupid portfolio to build and my paintings had to stick to this really limited list of what was acceptable. The focus of my paintings had to be on techniques like perspective and composition, reflections, vanishing points, shadows, and space, blah, blah, blah.

I had to have that portfolio to get into the program, and especially because I was applying for the National Scholarship, but all I really wanted to do was just paint what was in my soul.

It was the first time, too, that I felt like the drugs were making me…I don't know…like, numb. Like there was somehow a block between my brain and my head. I know that sounds lame, but that's the only way I can describe it. It wasn't blocked by the black cells—I hadn't had them for a long time, but I just felt like if I could stop taking the medicines then it would be easier for the ideas in my brain to get to my hands so I could be more creative.

Besides, I was so much better. I didn't get all depressed anymore and I was, um, happy I guess, so I really didn't need to take them anymore, but Dr. Anderson told me I had to take them, and even though I didn't want to, Nana made sure I took them every day, twice a day.

But then...Nana died. She died on Saturday, July lst. Happy fucking Canada Day.

The next two months were unbelievable and, really, I don't remember a lot of it. One day Nana and I were sitting there all excited because I got into Western--and the next day she's dead, and Angela and Mrs. Margalis are working together, and before I know it, the house is sold, I'm renting a little apartment in Somerset Place and I got so fucked up that I had to go to the hospital. Dr. Anderson changed my medicine and although I got to go to my little apartment in Somerset Place, I felt like a fucking zombie for the rest of the summer, and my life was just--gone.

But then, in September, I got to university and I kinda got my shit together and Dr. Anderson took me off some of the meds that seemed to zap me so much, switched around some other ones, and I actually started, like, living again.

They hooked me up with a counsellor at the university, too, and he was amazing. For being an old guy, he was kinda like the Energizer Bunny. He did all his own university stuff and he still had time to call me to make sure I was at class and he'd ask if I was still taking my medication, and he even

Lorrie Werden

gave me his cell phone number so I could call him whenever I needed to. I called him a lot in September and October and he was like, so awesome. He helped keep me organized and helped me remember where I was supposed to be and he helped me photocopy my class schedule so I had lots of copies of it in my apartment and in my binders and in my locker. I called him, "My Man," 'cause he had an unusual Ukrainian name that I really didn't understand when he introduced himself at our first meeting, and then I was too embarrassed to ask him, later, how to pronounce Mychajlo after I had read it on his desk name plate.

And Angela came a lot, too. I saw her several times every week. I'd go to her office or she'd come to my apartment to check it out and make sure it was clean and stuff, but sometimes, even when I didn't have an appointment, we'd meet at the Tim's on Oxford Street and we were just like two friends meeting for a coffee and talking about stuff. She would call me, too, and she'd 'pop over' sometimes on her way home from work and it was, I don't know, nice, I guess.

Then, everything just kinda clicked into place for me and I got into the routine of school and into the routine of getting groceries and washing my clothes and cleaning my apartment. After about November, I don't think I even called My Man again, and it was in November, too, that Angela was crazy busy planning her wedding and I got really busy with mid-terms so I didn't see her much after that, either, except for our scheduled appointments—but even those didn't seem to happen very often.

Black Blood

But by then—it didn't matter 'cause I'd met Corey and Oh. My. God. When we first met, it was like unbelievable magic. I was SO into my art and he was taking psychology and philosophy and we'd have these huge discussions about what my pictures meant and how awesome my creative mind was and what the symbolism was behind the paintings, and his insight into my art just blew me away. He really understood it. He didn't ever say any shit like, "Oh, isn't that a nice picture!" He'd say more in-depth stuff like, "The dark lines here indicate the fury that you feel when you think about your life. It's your way to release your anger for the trauma you suffered." Whatever. I just liked to get high with him, fuck him, and paint.

I did a pretty good job keeping up with all my assignments until about Christmas. I got through my mid-term exams OK, but after that, I just didn't feel like listening to everybody tell me what I had to study or what I had to paint. So, during the Christmas break, I wanted to really concentrate on my painting and to just let my creative juices flow, so I stopped taking my meds.

I was really kinda pissed off right then, too, 'cause Corey went home for the Christmas break and Dr. Anderson went to Florida and Angela went to Jamaica to get married and I was just, like, all alone. They all gave me about a dozen different phone numbers of people I could call if I got "into crisis," but, what the hell? I didn't know any of those people. Do you know how much time it would take to try to explain to those people who I was and why I was calling and what was wrong with me? Fuck that. I just stayed at my apartment and painted.

And then, it was like, I just got so into the painting. And I was feeling so good, and I'd get high, and I'd paint, and then I'd feel even better. And, soon, all I thought about was painting.

And, soon, I stopped eating.

And I stopped showering.

And I stopped everything except painting. I must have done about fifteen different canvases over those three weeks, and, oh, my God; they were all so awesome. Every single one of them was different and inspired and they each held such a different story. I couldn't wait for Corey to get back so he could see them and so we could talk about them and so he could tell me what part of my psyche I was exploring when I painted them and so we could get high and fuck, and so I could paint some more.

He was supposed to come back to residence on January the fifth and I waited all weekend for him to come over, but he didn't. So I called him on Monday and I told him how much painting I'd done and that I wanted him to see them.

We talked for a while but he sounded so different on the phone. But he kept asking me what was wrong with me and I asked him what was wrong with him because he didn't sound like the Corey I knew. Anyway, he came over that night and he walked into the apartment and he asked me what the fuck had happened and I looked around the place and I didn't know what he meant, and he said he had to go, and I just told him to get the fuck out of my house and I slammed the door.

And then I turned around and looked at my apartment.

And it was a disaster.

And I hadn't even realized it looked like that. And I called Corey and I told him I was sorry and he said that his parents were pissed at him because his grades sucked and that he had to get his shit together and concentrate on his studies and that he wouldn't be able to see me anymore.

And I felt the knife enter my heart.

He told me, too, that he was worried about me 'cause he thought there was something wrong with me.

And the knife twisted in my heart.

And I wondered how different I was that even though I'd never told him I was bipolar and suffered from depression and anxiety, he knew there was something wrong with me. And I remembered the times when we were together and I'd start to get manic, and he'd say we needed to get stoned and he'd pull out a joint and the buzz would quiet me. And I remembered the other times, when I already felt like I was stoned and just sat on the couch, and he'd bring the blow and we'd get high and we'd fuck our brains out and lie together, his arms around me, holding me, loving me. But who was gonna fuck me now that there was something wrong with me?

And the knife turned again and sliced my heart in half.

And when I hung up the phone…I don't really know what happened after that. Everything was just a blur. I know I took a shower and I ate a container of yogurt. I did a load of laundry because I'd been wearing the same clothes for about a week. I cleaned all my brushes and I wiped down my easel. I cleaned up the paint that was all over the floor and I put the paintings by the door so I could take them to Yvonne, but somehow, they had lost their luster.

And then I sat down on the floor and flattened my hand against my left tit to try to stop my sliced up heart from falling out of my chest—and I cried. And I cried.

And I cried.

And I never saw Corey again.

And I never got high again.

And I stopped going to school. And I lost my scholarship. And I had nothing left.

And Dr. Anderson's office called me and I could hear my voice on the answering machine telling them that I was "away from the phone" and I could hear them tell me that I had missed my appointment and my sliced up heart screamed at the phone for someone to please come to me. But I couldn't leave the floor.

And then Angela called and left a message. And another one. And another one until the answering machine had no more space, but I couldn't answer the phone or call her back 'cause I was glued to the floor.

And when she finally came over and let herself in with the key that I had given her, I was just laying there. I had become a board in the floor…and she called 9-1-1.

And they took me to the hospital.

And I knew, for sure, that I'd fucked up.

– 13 –

A Matter of Self-Control

Elizabeth thought she'd have the luxury of sleeping in once she got home, but the habit of waking before 7:00 a.m. had ingrained itself into her body while she was at the halfway house, and it reared its ugly head now. She tried turning over and going back to sleep, but she had to pee, so she got up and went to the bathroom. When she was done, she walked back down the hallway toward her bedroom, but she saw the sun peeking around the corner of the full-length windows downstairs, its rays spreading across the floor like melted butter, and she knew she had to go there.

She grabbed a large cushion from her bed and carried it downstairs. She plunked it on the floor, right in the middle of a ray of sunshine, and lowered herself onto it. She closed her eyes and let the warmth sink into her. She had missed this so much while she was away. The halfway house was shrouded by blinds and drapery to ensure the privacy of the women who resided there. Even on the brightest of days, it was dark inside and all the lights were turned on to give the illusion that there was natural light coming in. Nothing could replace real sunshine though, and right now, she just wanted to be swallowed up by its warmth. She shifted her hips off the pillow, lowered herself onto her side, and gathered the pillow into her arms. She fluffed it under her head and brought her knees up toward her chest, wrapping herself around the cushion. She nestled her head against the silkiness of the fabric and, if she had been a cat, she most assuredly would have been purring.

She lay there basking in the sunshine, enjoying its affection, for what seemed like only a miniscule amount of time, but it must have been much longer, for her stomach began to growl and she realized she was starving. She extended her legs and stretched them out, flexing her toes and heels, encouraging mobility to go there. She arched her back and stretched her arms up over her head, her hands pushing the pillow along the floor as she elongated her body, flooding it with an odd combination of sexuality, relaxation, and energy. She smiled.

She lifted her body into a standing position and started to formulate her plan for the day. Yesterday, Sunday, she had not followed any routine. She unpacked her painting paraphernalia and put them into the cupboards, or onto the shelves, where they belonged. She swept up the dust bunnies that had collected while she had been away, then stared out the windows, looking north, as she sipped coffee after coffee. Surprisingly, given the amount of caffeine she had consumed, she needed a nap in the afternoon, so she curled up on the loveseat, the only piece of furniture on the first floor, and snuggled into the darkness. When she awoke, she made a salad as directed on the menu plan, but she wasn't really hungry so most of the salad went into the garbage can. She felt quite giddy. While it may have been the impact of caffeine, she felt a closer kinship to this edginess as being the creativity bubbling within her. It was festering. It was there and she would just have to wait until it was ready to manifest itself.

That was yesterday. Today, she felt the need to stick to the routine that Doctor Almighty had approved. First, breakfast, then—she shrugged her shoulders with excitement—oh, what the hell, absolutely no drugs and absolutely no routine. She snickered as she anticipated the creativity that would hopefully overcome her. It was always a crap shoot when she went off the meds—she could go up or down—but somehow, today, she knew she'd go up because she felt *good* and she felt even better knowing that soon, she would be able to release the images trapped in her brain.

She went into the kitchen and stood in front of the coffee maker Yvonne had bought for her. Elizabeth had never tasted good coffee before she met Yvonne. Nana's beverage of choice had been tea, but she did keep a glass jar of instant coffee granules in the cupboard just in case any visitor wanted a cup of coffee. Of course, except for Father Michaels who was a tea drinker himself, no one was ever a visitor at their house (social workers did not count as visitors), so by the time Elizabeth was 17, that jar had been there for about five years, still awaiting its inaugural launch. On a whim, Elizabeth had taken it for a test drive. She broke the seal on the Holy Grail jar, made a cup of coffee according to the instructions, and discovered that she liked its taste. A few months later, when Yvonne came to pick up a canvas, Elizabeth proudly asked if she'd like a cup of coffee. Yvonne agreed, but when Elizabeth pulled out the glass jar, Yvonne declined and joked that she'd have to introduce Elizabeth to "real" coffee. A few weeks later, she did. The Java Hut, Timothy's, Starbuck's, and a little restaurant called the Red Rooster in Lambeth, all had excellent coffee of which Elizabeth soon became a fan. Of course, she could still swill it with Tim Horton's coffee when meeting Angela, but she discovered that purchasing Kona beans, grinding them herself, and brewing her own coffee beat a double-double any day.

The machine mattered, too, and Yvonne, as a housewarming gift, had bought her the Flavia Fusion. The uniquely sculpted machine stood on her counter now, and Elizabeth walked over to it, pulled out the water reservoir, carried it to the sink, and filled it up to the 2-cup line. She replaced it back into the machine then opened the freezer to look at her selection of fresh coffee beans. Hmm. What did she feel like today? Columbian? Peruvian? Hawaiian? No…Sumatra. Definitely Sumatra; something rich, something earthy.

While the coffee was dripping, she returned the bag of beans to the freezer and turned her attention to making breakfast. She spread an even coat of cottage cheese onto a slice of toast and, when the 'ready' light flickered green, she pulled the small pot of coffee from its burner and poured the hot liquid into her mug. She stirred the coffee, tapped the spoon twice on the side of the mug, and deposited the spoon into the sink. She slid her right hand under the paper towel to carry the toast, picked up the coffee in her left hand, and walked back to her cushion in the middle of the floor.

The sun had shifted itself so it was once again showering the cushion with light and she lowered herself onto the warm pillow. She put her coffee cup onto the hardwood floor and used both hands to raise the slice of toast. Holding the paper towel tight against her chin, she began to nibble at the toast. She started at the corner, eating only the crust and rotating the paper towel so she could eat it all the way around. In her mind, the bread had an invisible line that spiralled from the exterior edge of the bread, moving inward, around and around toward the centre of the slice. It reminded her of the ornaments she made as a child, cutting a small piece of paper into one continuous circle that, once unfurled, would stretch from the ceiling all the way down to the floor. By eating the toast and cottage cheese in continuous, little bites, and swallowing at regular intervals, the bread would settle gently into her stomach to recreate the solid piece of toast it had once been.

Camouflaging the masticated toast was a trick she liked to pull on her stomach, and a lesson learned after a biology class in secondary school wherein Mr. Silverstein, the biology teacher, had told her that the digestive system was the only part of the body that was considered truly autonomous—the only part of her body over which she had no control, the only part of her body that could "function in isolation" because it had as many neurons as her entire spinal cord did. When he said the digestive tract was the *only* part of her body over which she had no control, she absolutely knew that wasn't true. She also couldn't control the black cells, nor could she control the depression or the mania; now this teacher was telling her she couldn't control her stomach either? She could feel the hairs on the back of her neck bristle in anger at the thought that there was yet one more part of her body, of her own anatomy, over which she had no control.

Well, you know what? Fuck that. She might not be able to control this autonomous nervous system shit, but she could certainly outsmart it. By re-forming the entire, whole, thick slice of toast, her stomach would think an extraordinary amount of acid and effort were required to dissolve it. The gastric juices, hiding within the layers of her stomach, hidden there like snipers, received the message that there was an invader in their stomach's fortress. "How big is the item that has entered our cavern?" they would murmur amongst themselves. "How many of us do we need to send to disseminate the item? Oh, it's a big invader—we need to emit a lot of juice. Send out all the troops!" Elizabeth sat so still that she could feel the molecules ooze out of the lining of her stomach, slinking their way toward the bread and cottage cheese. There were thousands of them. Thousands of cells of acid, advancing toward the intruder, but, when the stomach juices reached the invader and started to break it up, they would soon discover that the bread was not one whole piece as perceived, but merely thousands and thousands of crumbs that were already well on their way to being digested. She could see the cells of acid in her stomach sharing looks of 'what the fuck' on their little acidic faces and just milling about in her stomach with nothing to do.

Once all the acidic juices were in this vulnerable position, Elizabeth grabbed her coffee and gulped it as quickly as she could. The liquid hit her stomach all at once and with such force that the remnants of her breakfast formed into a tidal wave that sloshed from side to side in her stomach, forcing the particles of acid back into the lining of her stomach. The stickiness of the cottage cheese and the liquid of the coffee mixed together and immediately created a glue-like substance that pinned the acidic molecules against the mucosa, trapping them from being autonomous, stopping them from doing their job and essentially putting Elizabeth in control over her own autonomic nervous system. Controlling the uncontrollable. She smiled and chuckled to herself. Control.

Her thoughts turned to Doctor Almighty and she wondered what he would think about her need to control right now. He'd make her think about the recent changes that had transpired over the past 72 hours. He'd lead her to the conclusion that, although she was glad to be back in her own apartment, striking out again on her own was a bit frightening, and even though she portrayed the epitome of bravery, there was still a little girl inside who wanted, and needed, the guidance of people that she trusted. Whatever. She didn't need people. She just needed freedom.

And she needed to move. Thoughts and ideas were starting to come to her. She felt antsy and wanted to *do* something. Crumpling the paper towel, she carried it and the mug into the kitchen. She placed the mug in the sink and threw the paper towel into the trash can. She turned toward the stairs and bounded up them two at a time. When she reached the top, she stripped off her t-shirt and underwear and left them on the landing. She walked into the bathroom and turned on the rainforest shower head. She stood outside the shower for several minutes, letting the water run over her hand, turning the tap back and forth to ensure the water was at just the right temperature before stepping into the marble stall. The water felt exactly the same as her body temperature. As the water poured over her, it was barely noticeable as it fell against her. Anyone else entering the shower would find it too cold, but Elizabeth knew this was the right temperature. She knew that many women relished in taking long, hot showers, but she never understood the fascination with being in the water for such an extended period of time. Of course, Elizabeth did not even have her first shower until she was 14. Nana had continued to bathe her until she was 10, and when Elizabeth took over that area of personal hygiene, she continued to wash herself in the same fashion that Nana used, scouring, heavy passes with the washcloth, as if she were a dirty shirt being pushed around on an old washboard.

Elizabeth's first shower was in ninth grade and was an experience that shaped the course of future bathing. It was the second week of school. During a Phys Ed class in the first week, they had discussed the curriculum for the school year and Ms. Matheson performed a Body Mass Index for each girl. The teacher declared them all out of shape, and indicated that their first classes in the gym would be aerobics. So there they were, 20 obeying pre- and post-pubescent girls huffing and puffing in their little black shorts and 'Warrior' t-shirts, sweat dripping down their faces and building in their pits as they flung their arms and stomped their feet trying to keep up to Ms. Matheson's cries of, "And one. And two. And three. Arms up! And one. And two. And three."

When class was finished, they herded back to the change room, grabbed towels and entered the shower room. They stood there, all 20 girls lined up, facing an open room with only 10 shower heads. Claire Manders was the first to strip. She hung her clothes and towel on the hooks situated on the wall behind where they were standing and walked proudly to the shower. Claire was tanned and trim and acted as if she had bathed in front of people before. She turned the water on and by the time she had soaked her hair, eight other girls had stripped and joined her. They laughed and giggled; tossed bars of soap to one another, and carried on conversations as if they were fully clothed. One by one, 19 girls completed their hurried showers and returned to the change room to dry off and re-dress before lunch. Elizabeth listened as their voices faded when they left the change room. Someone had left one of the showers running and Elizabeth removed her clothes and stepped gingerly forward to the cascading drops. She extended her hand toward the water but once it lashed at her skin, her arm ricocheted back as if she had touched poison. The water was much, much too hot, but she discovered that she could regulate the temperature so that it coincided with the needs of her body. She knew that a hot bath could bring the black cells so she loathed having her body submerged in hot water, but this intermittent dripping was nice. She could step in and out of the downpour as she needed for the perfunctory necessity of cleansing, but the water did not enclose her; it merely took away the sweat and dirt and carried it down the drain. She could regulate the length of time in which she remained in the water, too, so her showers were quick enough to avoid the black cells, but long enough to ensure social acceptability. Brilliant!

Elizabeth was so fascinated with this new concept of showering, that it wasn't until Ms. Matheson returned from her lunch duty to angrily find her still in the shower, that Elizabeth realized for how long she had been exploring this newness. She quickly dried off, dressed, and got to her afternoon class on time, but not before realizing that today, in school, she had actually learned something of immense value.

Back in her marble ensuite, she showered exceptionally quickly, just long enough to remove the bed-head hairdo and to do a little personal hygiene. She turned the water tap off and grabbed the smaller towel from the bar positioned just outside the shower. She bent forward at the waist and flipped her shoulder-length hair forward so she could wrap the towel around her head. She stepped out of the shower and removed the blanket towel from the heated rack, patted her arms and legs dry, then wrapped its softness around her body. She padded back to her bedroom, grabbed paint plastered cut-off jeans from a drawer and threw them on. A once white, over-the-shoulder t-shirt was thrown over her shrouded head to complete her outfit for the day. After a quick rubbing of her head, she ran a brush through her hair and pulled it back into a ponytail.

She was ready to work.

–14–

Never Nana

I had a really hard time after Trevor and I broke up. After the brief visit from Father Michaels, I tried as hard as I could to get up for my grandmother, but I just could not. Being unable to do as she commanded just seemed to be one more thing for which I felt badly and the blanket of sadness that covered me then became a closed coffin that completely immobilized me. The four days spent in bed turned into six days, and when Nana could smell my accidents all the way down the stairs, she called for an ambulance. I don't remember being taken to the hospital; I don't remember meeting Dr. Anderson or Angela, the social worker. I don't even remember coming home, but I do remember Nana taking really, really good care of me.

While I was in the hospital, she got rid of my soiled mattress and replaced it with the one from her old bed so that when I got home, I was welcomed by a freshly made, nice, clean bed. She made sure I took my new medicines every day and I know she was worried about me because for five full days after I got home from the hospital, she made the trip upstairs to look after me. She brought me my drugs, she helped me get out of bed to go to the bathroom, and she made me toast for breakfast, a sandwich for lunch, and Swanson's TV dinners at night.

On the sixth morning of being home, I surprised her by sneaking downstairs to the kitchen and putting the tea kettle on for her morning cup of tea. When I took it to her, she reached her speckled hand up to my face and touched my cheek. She didn't hold it there for very long, but in the brief moment that she touched me, I felt a ray of warmth that comforted me all the way through my body and snuggled itself into me like a warm heating pad. I looked into Nana's eyes but when she saw me searching her soul, trying to establish a relationship between us, her hand dropped from my face and the moment was broken. Nana never touched me like that again, but that was OK because she touched me when I needed it the most, when I needed a tangible lifeline between my shrivelled view of the world and the real world that awaited me.

During my time of recuperation, Nana eased off on the housecleaning, too. She still swept the floor and scrubbed the kitchen countertops after breakfast, but she didn't clean in there again until after supper. The daily rituals of cleaning all the rooms in the house ceased, too. Since she had moved downstairs, she no longer cleaned her old bedroom. Three years ago, when she left that room for the final time to move

Black Blood

downstairs, she firmly closed the door and we both heard the fierce 'click' that resonated as if the room decided to lock itself off from the rest of the house—and that was the way it had remained.

She'd stopped cleaning the upstairs bathroom too, except when I was sick, but she only did that twice. Once I was well enough, it became my job again. Since she wasn't cleaning and scouring the house so much, the majority of her day was freed up and she began spending that free time outdoors. I don't know when she did these things, but she planted purple and yellow pansies beside the back porch and she hung a bird feeder from a cup hook screwed into the ceiling of the porch. She asked Mr. Watson, the next door neighbour, to carry an old metal rocker up from the basement and he placed it on the pad of shaded concrete that was just below the back porch steps. Nana sat and rocked and watched the birds come and go from the birdfeeder. When the seeds had all been eaten, she'd take the broom and sweep up the leftover shells off the concrete pad, then carry the full dustpan to be emptied into the garbage can. She'd refill the feeder from the bag of birdseed that was kept in a big Rubbermaid container under the porch, and I'd hear her grunt as she lifted off the cinder block that she kept on the lid so squirrels and mice couldn't get into the seed for themselves.

For many days after I got home from the hospital, I sat outside with her. Nestled onto the bottom step of the porch with an old throw pillow propped behind me, I sat and watched the birds while the music from my CD player blasted Motley

Lorrie Werden

Crue and Slipknot through my new earbuds. In the evening, we moved into the living room and Nana and I sat together on the couch and ate Habitant minestrone soup while we watched Wheel of Fortune and Jeopardy. After we ate, we took turns between sweeping and scrubbing the floor, and washing the dishes and countertop.

Two weeks after I got home, I started seeing Dr. Anderson again. Every Thursday I walked up Hamilton Road to take the city bus from our corner to his outpatient clinic on Grosvenor Street. I don't remember our sessions together. I don't remember what we talked about or what he said to me, but I do remember that I started to feel happy again.

When I was well enough to return to school in September, I had to start Grade 11 all over again, but this time I took different courses. I still had to take the required English, Math, and Science, but the Resource Teacher helped me discover the Visual Arts program. I had always liked to draw, but being introduced to the creativity and freedom of painting unleashed some intrinsic talent within me that no one knew I had. The paintings that flowed from my gut and onto the canvas had been with me for years—but now I had a venue in which to explore and illustrate them.

Although I still had some emotional difficulties through the eleventh grade, my teachers encouraged and supported me. At school, I was able to create several good pieces and I continued to develop my skills and learned to recognize my own unique ability of having the canvas speak to me. My art teachers, and by now Angela, who had also become one of my best supporters, helped me enter and win several art competitions. I'd been introduced to Yvonne, too, and she was showing a great interest in my work.

Most surprisingly, though, was the way Nana responded to my painting. Several weeks before I turned 18, she called Salvation Army and had them remove the furniture from her enshrined bedroom. She hired a handyman too, but the work he did was just as secreted as when she had her little bathroom downstairs created. I was not privy to why the renovations were being made and frankly, I was too busy in my own life to pay attention to the production anyway.

I spent more time away from home than at home that year. Every day after school, I rode the bus home, but after a quick supper of cereal or frozen meat pies, I took the city bus back to the school where the principal allowed me a space to paint in the janitor's room. Clarence and Isabelle, the janitors, looked in on me periodically, but mostly, they left me alone so I could revel in the creation and experience of painting.

The routine of travelling back and forth between school and home changed though when I returned home on the occasion of my 18th birthday. Nana asked me to go into her old bedroom and bring down a box of old photographs from the closet. Begrudgingly, because I really just wanted to eat and get back to the school, I climbed the stairs to retrieve her stupid pictures. I stomped up the stairs and heaved open the door to her old room. Expecting to rush in, go over to the closet and grab the pictures, my body reacted instead as if it had slammed into a brick wall, jarred to a stop.

Lorrie Werden

I was stunned by what filled my vision. Unable to breathe, I struggled to comprehend what had happened in this room. New vinyl flooring had been put down in place of the worn, threadbare carpet. A fresh coat of neutral paint replaced the dated floral wallpaper, and not only had the single bulb ceiling light been changed to a pendant-dropped fixture, but there were now two floor lamps in the corner, and an angle-poised lamp atop a small work bench. As unexpected as this view was, it began to make sense to me when I saw what was standing below the new ceiling light. There, with a small red bow on its ledge, was a brand new MABEF M-06 Studio Easel. Gingerly, as if walking on the floor might awake me from this dream, I crossed the room to the easel. I recognized it immediately as one of the models that Francis Bacon used when he painted. We had learned about him in Art History class and although I didn't really like his provocative, meat-inspired art, I felt a kinship of inspiration with him. I memorized the words he said about a painting he had done in 1948: "It came to me as an accident… suddenly the line that I had drawn suggested something totally different and out of this suggestion arose this picture. I had no intention to do this picture; I never thought of it in that way. It was like one continuous accident mounting on top of another." He felt as I felt—that a painting started as just one small speck on the canvas, one small speck of inspiration, and then it just created itself, spurred on by unstoppable forces coming from deep within my body and my soul.

I drew closer to the easel. In revered wonder, I sank to my knees and lowered my gaze, humbled by its presence. I reached my shaking hands out in trepidation to touch the highly oiled beech wood and I clasped the frame lovingly. My hands then travelled down toward the base of the frame and unlocked the casters that held it steady in its place. Unleashed, the easel turned easily around in front of me and I watched it twirl and whirl as a fashion designer might watch a runway model displaying his newest creation. I caressed the fine straight lines of the frame and my eyes travelled upward, taking in its height and its sturdiness. I opened the little drawer below the canvas ledge and listened with rapture to the whoosh sound it made as it slid back into place.

I understood then, that Nana had created this room for me as my own private creative oasis, but I could not comprehend why she would do this for me. She had never shown any interest in art—we had no pictures on our walls, not even family photos. Did she appreciate my art? Was there a connection between us of which I had no knowledge, a commonality that somehow blended our souls?

I went back downstairs and sat beside her on the couch. I didn't know what to say, how to thank her. I sat with tears rolling down my cheeks wanting to hug her and pull her to her feet so we could jump up and down together in excitement, but I was afraid to touch her, afraid that if I did so, I would be rejected and she would change her mind about giving me the easel. So, I just sat there, sniffling a little as snot threatened to roll out my nose.

Nana broke the silence. Staring straight ahead at the TV screen she said, "There is no box of pictures in that closet,

Lorrie Werden

Elizabeth. There never has been. All the pictures you need are in your head. Your mother was always trying to create something beautiful with all her cutting and pasting, but you actually can. You have a real talent, Elizabeth—Yvonne said so—and she said you needed that easel. You are spending valuable painting time travelling back and forth on that bus. Just this last time, I want you to go back to school and get your paints. You have a place to paint here now." She stood and made her way to the kitchen door. Before she escaped into the room she said, "I'll have supper ready for you when you get back. Hurry on, now."

I moved my paints home but we never again spoke of the renovations she made to her old bedroom. Nor did we speak of my painting. Her connection to my world of painting was through Yvonne whom Nana would call to ask how I was doing with my painting and if I had sold any. Nana never entered her old bedroom to look at my work. She did not allow me to show any of my paintings to her. If she wanted to see them, she would attend, for a few brief moments, a viewing at Yvonne's gallery or look at them in the art auction magazines Yvonne would leave on the end table near Nana's chair.

Never again did I feel any connection with my Nana the way I had for my 18th birthday. Never did I actually thank her for the easel. Never. Never.

– 15 –

Inspiration Cometh

Once her hair was caught back in the ponytail, Elizabeth skipped down the stairs into her work space ready to unleash the images that were starting to saturate her brain. She looked at the primed canvases lined up along the windows on the east wall. There were probably 20 of them: blank, white, big, small, all staring back at her, each one screaming to her, "Pick me! Pick me!" She walked beside them and touched each one as she passed it. Some, she merely ran her finger along the top edge, just enough to acknowledge it. With the larger ones, she placed the flat of her palm, hand still and steady on each canvas, searching her soul to see if this was the right one. She finally settled on a larger one. It was three feet by five feet. She slid it out from behind another one and gave it prominence in front of some smaller frames. It had called out to her, beckoned her. She dropped to her knees in front of it and closed her eyes. She lifted her arms in front of her and placed both palms on the rough canvas fabric. Again, she held her hands still and steady. With her eyes closed, she scanned the myriad of images in her head. She focused on the lights, the colours, and the images, and allowed them to be free. "Go," she silently said to the images. "Go to the canvas." She did not know which ones would go to the canvas. She did not know which images would become her next painting, but she did know they would reveal themselves eventually.

As she knelt, her shoulders felt suddenly warm and she knew the images were beginning to move out from her brain, trying to reach the canvas. Her arms began to tingle as the yet unknown images travelled toward her hands. Once the images got there, then she would be able to release them onto the canvas. Her fingers started to twitch when the colours and textures she felt in her hands started to form a picture in her mind's eye.

She had to move quickly now. She opened her eyes and went to the closet that housed her larger painting supplies. She pulled out a paint-splattered tarpaulin that was hanging on a hook. She shook it until it had unfolded itself and, once it had opened, she threw it on the floor and began smoothing it out. She could feel the excitement rising inside her. This painting was strong in her hands and they felt heavy holding the images. She must get the painting out of herself and onto the canvas.

She returned to retrieve the canvas, carried it to the centre of the room, and placed it on the tarp. Retracing her steps back to the cupboard, she pulled out a stack of eight empty, one-gallon pails, then closed the closet door. From the nearby shelves, she removed large cans of interior latex paints and set them on the floor. This painting did not want to be in oils; this was a resilient painting that was going to need lots of paint, lots of motion, and begged for a fluid statement. She could get that from the acrylic resin in these paints. Oils would be too slow. They would not dry quickly enough; they would be too thick and bulky.

Even the brushes she chose were big. From the shelves, she picked up a milk crate filled with large brushes and placed them beside the paints. She loved these brushes. She ran her right hand over the tips of the brushes to tease them with the images she held in her palm. She played with the synthetic filaments and could feel the subtle differences between them. Some brushes were made only of nylon or only of polyester; some were a combination of the two. The bristled brushes were made of natural ox hair and were sturdy and strong. She would use these to put strength into the picture.

She returned to the closet and retrieved the drill to which was attached what looked like a long-stemmed egg beater. She untangled the long electric cord and plugged it in. She set the mixer on the floor and returned again to the cupboard to grab a five-gallon pail. She carried it over to the industrial sink that was to the right of the windows—an addition she had had installed when she first bought the condo—and filled it with warm water and soap. As she carried it back to where she had placed the mixer, she also grabbed another tarp out of the cupboard and, once straightened out, she placed her mixing and painting equipment onto it. She opened the can of robin's egg blue paint and placed the beater into it. Using a very low speed, she zapped the trigger in three pulses to blend the paint. She cautiously lifted the drill to look at the paint, replaced the beater, and zapped it again until it was well blended. She quickly placed the beater into the pail of warm, soapy water and rinsed it off. She returned to the pail of paint and poured a quantity into one of the smaller containers she had placed beside the canvas.

Elizabeth repeated this procedure with the other paints, stirring them and pouring small amounts into the smaller receptacles. She was quivering with excitement as she placed these pots around the perimeter of the canvas. She reached into the carton of brushes and selected one. Her hand shook as it held the brush; the need to paint was that strong. The life of the painting was oozing from her hand and into the paintbrush and it needed to get onto the canvas. Elizabeth freed her mind and let the painting begin. Deftly, the brush was dunked into a container of paint and the race began. Broad strokes of one colour, a grab for another brush. More paint. Mores strokes. Dabbing and swirls. Moving around the canvas. Upwards strokes mixed with tiny jabs of colour made with smaller brushes.

She flew to the cupboard and retrieved more empty containers. Without complete comprehension of her actions, she blended and mixed a multitude of colours. Her hands flew across the canvas. The excitement had built to a frenzy now and Elizabeth painted with abandon. The sun was shining directly on the painting and Elizabeth could see the dust mites dancing in the air, illuminated by the sun's rays. They were begging to be part of the painting. They swirled around in front of Elizabeth and flitted from her paintbrush to hover over the canvas. She swooped the paint brush into the air to capture the mites and, drawing them downward, she painted them into the canvas.

Elizabeth painted for hours but was unaware of the span of time. She stretched her arms and elongated her body to fill every bit of the canvas with the imagery that flowed through her. From brush to canvas, then into the water, a different brush, a different stroke, dipping into the different colours, mixing their hues. More strokes, faster and faster, then abruptly stopping so that she could grab a smaller brush to create a hidden, intimate detail. Then again, a flurry of activity. She laughed and screamed as the picture erupted from her body and she shuddered with orgasmic force as sweeps of the paint brushes tickled the canvas. With each flick of her brush, paint splattered far beyond the reaches of the tarpaulin and landed on the floor, sprayed across the windows, and landed on Elizabeth. She didn't notice. She had no separate life now. The life was in the painting. It had become vibrantly alive and was pulling her into it. She ceased being Elizabeth, and in spirit, she was miraculously transported into the painting. Once her soul was inside the painting, she was the conductor, directing the flow of the paint from within the canvas. Although she could will the paint to go exactly where it belonged, she did not feel in control of the painting. The control was at the mercy of her energetic hands, her frenzied mind, and her inner, independent being, and she painted until the images had been completely drained from her brain.

Once she was back inside her body, she realized she was panting heavily and perspiration dripped from her body. She gulped for air and wondered how long it had been since she had drawn in a breath. Her heart was pounding and her arms were now aching to be silent at her sides. She was spent. She was getting a headache and was suddenly, overwhelmingly, unbelievably, tired. This was how it always was after an inspired painting. She needed to sleep now to gain back some of the energy expended on the painting. With an intense heaviness, she picked up the paint brushes and carried them over to the sink. She didn't care that paint still dripped from the brushes and onto the floor. It was easy enough to clean the water-based paint from the floor and from the brushes. She cleaned the bristles but could not muster the strength to empty and clean the small containers of paint. She had used most of the paint she had prepared in them anyway and tomorrow she would throw these containers in the garbage. What she needed now was rest.

Without even looking at the painting, Elizabeth walked past the wall of windows and climbed the staircase to her bedroom. She stripped off her clothes, slunk into bed, and fell asleep instantly.

– 16 –

And Goeth

Tuesday came and went. Wednesday came and went. Late on Thursday afternoon, Elizabeth crawled out of bed and made her way to the shower. Under the tepid water, she washed off the days-old paint using brisk, hard strokes of the washcloth. She was undertaking each movement by rote memory. Her mind was just barely there, just barely alive. The water and the scrubbing brought her more into the present and by the time she had finished drying herself off, she was cognizant of where she was and what she needed to do to become human again.

She dressed in baggy sweatpants and an extra-large t-shirt and began to descend the staircase to the living room. As her hand slid along the bannister, she felt the raised droplets of dried paint that had been flung there during her painting session. This led her eyes to travel to the canvas languishing in the middle of the room below her. With one look, she could feel her heart start to swell. She could feel the energy of the painting calling to her. She flew down the rest of the stairs and rushed to the canvas. She reverently knelt before the painting and allowed her eyes to sweep over her creation. It was miraculous. Although the acrylic paint lay smooth and liquid on the canvas, there was so much depth in the painting that Elizabeth feared she could again be drawn into the actual canvas. Her eyes searched each stroke, each subtle nuance a brush had made, while her mind undertook the task of envisioning a name for the painting.

This was a painting in blues and browns. In front of a dark, angry sky, a roaring ocean tossed a sailing ship to and fro over waves and foam. Truly, there was so much movement in the painting that the ship appeared to be pitched from one wave to another. The water rolled before her eyes and she followed a cascading wave as it crashed into the ocean and flowed towards her. The multi-hued blues of the ocean water then became the beige-brown grains of sand that spread across the bottom of the canvas. There, buried within the hills of sand, were half-hidden skeletal bones. A tiny skull here, a broken femur there. There seemed to be hundreds of references to the dead of long ago and the name of the painting came to her straightaway, 'Shipwrecked.'

Elizabeth tenderly placed the canvas against her tucked-up knees and allowed her hand to trace the outlines of the waves and of the sand dunes. It was good. She was pleased. She stood up and carried the canvas to the easel. Carefully balancing it on the ledge, she placed it there so that she could step away from the imagery and look at it from a distance, to interpret it as a buyer might. As she moved away, the dominant strokes and hidden images became more integrated into the picture. She was not able to see the waves triumphantly gain their height on the canvas, nor could she hear the water as it lapped against the sand. By the time she had retreated five steps, the canvas contained just a painting. An excellent painting to be sure but, as with most of her pictures, the true beauty was seen upon close inspection. She loved this about her artwork. You could walk by any of her paintings and think, "Wow, that's awesome." Its appeal would then draw you closer, and the closer you came, the more you saw, the more the painting drew you into its intricacies and captured not only your imagination, but your soul as well. You became one with the setting and every single person who looked at any of her paintings, each felt a different emotional pull from the picture. Some were moved to tears. Some became peaceful and introspective. Some were angered. But regardless of the sentiments drawn from them, everyone loved her paintings and the reactions they induced.

Elizabeth smiled as she looked at the picture. Yvonne would love it, but Elizabeth was hesitant to telephone her about it just yet. She needed some time to break her own ties with the painting before she could release it into the world.

With the painting safely mounted on the easel, Elizabeth realized how hungry she was. She hadn't eaten for days and, now that the picture was out of her, she realized she was starving—famished! She trotted to the kitchen, ignoring the painted chaos she felt under her bare feet as she walked across the floorboards. She reached the refrigerator and threw open the door. There was a butterfly pork chop she could pop into the oven and, she determined with a certain degree of smugness, she could be eating a nice supper within 45 minutes. She grabbed a knife from the block and, with a flick of the wrist, sliced opened the cellophane wrapping surrounding the pork chop. With a fork wrestled from the utensil holder in the drawer, she pierced the chop and lifted it from its styrofoam cradle. She liked pork chops. They didn't ooze red blood when you pierced the raw meat. The same was true for chicken; but not true for beef. She rarely ate beef and if she did, she ensured that it was well, well-done. She hated, of course, the sight of any blood. Interestingly, though, when she was really free of the stabilizing drugs, there was a desire within her to demonstrate to herself that she had complete power over blood cells. To accomplish this, she would eat a steak, just to prove she could do it.

She thought back to her last bout of mania and how it had skipped all the usual patterned behaviours like eating a steak. The black cells had come very, very quickly. Her mania was also very short-lived that time and, once in the hospital, she spiralled quickly into a state of catatonia. She wondered fleetingly, as she held the pork chop high in the air, how her body would react this time by going off the medications, but she felt too happy and carefree to dwell on this mystery.

Black Blood

Upon hearing the 'ding' of the oven that stated, "I'm ready," she popped the dish into the now heated oven. She threw the styrofoam wrapping into the garbage (she was soon going to have to empty that) and turned her attention to making the required salad. With the head of lettuce on the chopping board, she placed her hand atop it and pushed down with all her weight to crush it against the wood. She flipped the head over and, with the seal of the root now broken, she pulled out the core and threw it, too, into the trash. She ripped four lettuce leaves from the head and chucked the rest of the green orb back into the fridge. Leaving the door wide open, she returned to the cutting board and, placing the four leaves one on top of the other, she rolled them up. With the chef's knife, she Pasquale Carpino'd the lettuce and laid the shards onto the left side of the plate. Three red, cherry tomatoes were retrieved from the countertop where they had flown when she fumbled to open their plastic container. She cut them in half, and threw them on the lettuce as she returned to the opened refrigerator to get the Italian dressing. Remaining in a bent-over position, she simultaneously slid the bottle along the counter towards the plate and pulled open one of the refrigerator bins from which she plucked a potato. She did a James Brown slide over to the sink, turned on the water, and scrubbed and scrubbed and re-scrubbed the potato, poked it again and again and again with a clean fork, and popped it into the microwave for six minutes.

Retrieving coffee beans from the freezer, she set to work making a cup of coffee and while it was brewing, her toes jumped against the floor in time to the drip, drip, drip of the machine. Once it was brewed and poured into a mug, Elizabeth tiptoed to the small dining area and placed the beverage on the Millennial dining set. While standing, she looked at the steaming brew, licked her lips, then took three quick gulps of the hot liquid.

When the oven timer went, she skipped back to the kitchen and stabbed at the offending buttons to stop the beeping sound. She threw open the door and stood back as the heat escaped into the room. With a mitted hand, she pulled the dish out of the oven, pushed the door closed with her right leg, then upturned the bakeware so the meat slid onto her plate. With the pork chop now settled, she opened the microwave oven door to rescue the wilted potato and flopped it between the salad and the chop. She flicked open the salad dressing, drowned the greens, grabbed a clean knife and fork from the drawer, and carried them with the plate to the table and sat down.

And she stared at the food. And she decided she definitely did not want to eat this. This was not going to satisfy her. Nope. Not tonight. Tonight she needed something else. Something exciting. Tonight, she needed to be filled. She needed to fill her stomach, her mind, and her body. She needed food and drink and music and sex. She started to feel an excitement bubble in her chest and her right leg began to jiggle under the table. She stood up, grabbed the plate of food and threw it all into the garbage. A glance at the wall clock told her it was nearly six o'clock. Soon, Richmond Street would be bursting with activity and she was going to be part of it!

Leaving the kitchen, she turned, leapfrogged up the stairs, and raced into the bathroom. She pulled the elastic from her hair, shook it out, and looked at it in the mirror. Good. It was nice and full and, when she ran the brush through it, it fell just right. It parted naturally on the left side and, when the hair draped forward over her forehead, she slipped the long bang sideways over her right ear. The slight curling of that piece of hair tucked nicely around her ear, while the rest of the hair bobbed gracefully at her shoulders. She grabbed some hairspray from under the sink and spritzed it along the front of her head.

She went then to her bedroom and sat down at the dressing table. From the drawer, she pulled out a make-up bag that contained a myriad of unused cosmetics. These, under the direction of Yvonne, had been purchased so that Elizabeth could get "dolled-up" for when she attended art events. That never, ever happened. The trepidation and anxiety that Elizabeth felt before those trials of terribleness well outweighed her desire to "look pretty" when she attended them. She was always too consumed with anxiety about her arrival, the people, the noise, the attention, the handshaking, and the well-wishers, to ever worry about what she looked like when she got there. Today, though, seemed like the day to give these bins of beauty a test drive.

Lorrie Werden

She dumped the paraphernalia of prettiness out of the bag and spread them on the make-up table in front of her. She opened every container and looked at the colours. Yvonne had once tried to show her how to use them and Elizabeth thought back on what she had been instructed. She found the bottle of foundation and popped open the top. She took a small, white, triangular sponge from its bag, and squeezed a glob of the foundation onto it. This, she then dabbed on her forehead, a bit under each eye, a daub on the end of her nose, and one on her chinny-chin-chin. She snickered at her spotted reflection in the mirror but then, with a fierce seriousness, drew her attention to the task at hand. With the sponge, she dragged the foundation across her face, connecting all the dots and feathering the liquid out so that it evenly covered her face. It really was just like painting, she thought, but on a much smaller canvas. Even putting on eye shadow was like painting, especially since it was done with a brush! She lifted up the square container that held four shimmering colours of eye shadow and pried open the lid. Yvonne said these colours would accentuate Elizabeth's blue eyes and, from an artistic point of view, Elizabeth had to agree. Starting with the deep taupe, Elizabeth applied a band of the colour in the crease of each eye. She followed that up with a dark brown triangle on the outside corners of her eyelids, then painted the soft peach colour across the rest of the eyelid. She got a different brush then, and lightly fanned it across the entirety of the closed lids to blend the colours. Once that was done, she used the iridescent off-white colour just under her eyebrows to "accentuate its natural shape." Whatever.

Elizabeth did not try to put on eyeliner; she knew she was too shaky to attempt that trick. She did, however, manage to finish each eye with a swipe of mascara on her eyelashes, and even applied a coating of lip gloss to her mouth. She looked at herself in the mirror. She wanted to look perfect for this evening and, gazing at her reflection, she liked what she saw.

Standing up from the tiny table, she rapidly stripped, and made her way to the closet. She picked a dress that Yvonne had made her buy for one of her private showings with the Governor from New South Wales. It was a sleeveless, flowing little number, but the top hugged in all the right places. Although Elizabeth was tiny, she had been given a good set of breasts that had begun to sprout when she was about 13. By the time she had that first shower in high school, they had developed into a set that the other girls had envied, and even now, free from the confines of a bra, they were taut and firm. She slipped the chemise over her naked body then reached into her underwear drawer for a pair of cream coloured, lacy, bikini undies and pulled them on.

Happiness formed in her chest and her smile came naturally as she caught a glimpse of herself in the mirror. Both her breathing and the beating of her heart quickened. She knew she was going to have a wonderful night. She gambolled over to the closet and knelt down before the few jumbled pairs of shoes. Like playing a game of concentration, she matched each pair to its partner before selecting a pair of kitten heel shoes that were purchased to match the dress. She slipped her bare feet into them then rummaged in the closet to find the matching purse. Its chain shoulder strap felt foreign to her as she put it over her head, cross-body style. It was not soft and comfortable like the strap of the big, blue, patchwork bag she usually carried, but she knew she'd get used to it. She retrieved her wallet from the big, blue granny bag, ensured there was still the wad of cash in there that she had acquired on one of last week's preparation outings, and transferred it into the slender purse. She threw the keyring with the code for the elevator, and the key for her apartment in there, too, and, after one more look in the mirror to satisfy her quest for perfection, she then dashed down the stairs. She let herself out of the apartment and stood in the hall, tapping her toes inside the shoes until the elevator arrived. She allowed the elevator to carry her to the lobby, waited impatiently for its sliding doors to open, bounced out of the now stopped elevator, and flew through the front door.

    She headed toward the bus stop on Pall Mall Street, but changed her mind and decided to walk the few blocks to downtown London. She headed east, then turned left onto Richmond Street. Not quite sure of where her final destination would be, she jaywalked across Richmond, dodging cars driving both north and south on the street as she went. She fell into the quick-step tempo of the people who were walking towards their own destinations. She might not be sure where she was going, but she was certainly glad to be out among the people, and she absorbed their energy and excitement.

As she walked, the June breeze washed over Elizabeth's face like one of her soft, sable paintbrushes, stroking her, lulling her. As she raised her hands to lovingly touch her face, she was suddenly, and unexpectedly, slapped by the thought of Nana's harsh washcloths washing her face over and over again—before she went to school, before she went outside to play, before she went to bed. Recalling this, her face suddenly felt raw and the once lulling breeze now felt as if it had cut deeply into her flesh. Removed from the blissfulness of the warm breeze, her arms instinctively wrapped around her body, cradling herself for security. She continued to walk but shuffled closer to the storefronts in an attempt to protect herself from her thoughts and to gain control of the moment. With her shoulder propped against the window of a store, she focused her eyes on the lines ahead of her in the sidewalk, but a childhood rhyme kept her steadfast in the moment of uncertainty. *Step on a crack, break your Nana's back. Step on a line, break your Nana's spine.*

When she began to have difficulty breathing, she realized that her arms were wrapped so tightly around her body that she was squeezing her ribcage. In fact, her hands had travelled so far around her back that she could very nearly touch her own spine. She loosened her grip, and took several deep breaths. As she continued to breathe, she became aware of the sensation of the soft, gentle fabric beneath her hands. She felt the way the dress hugged her body and this connection to the fabric brought her back into the moment. Her hands touched the fabric and she became aware of the way the dress clung closely to her skin and lay so smoothly against her body without any bra line to ripple the fabric. She took three more deep breaths and allowed herself to concentrate on her surroundings. With each breath, she became more aware, and more focused. She looked at the people around her and searched them for their energy. She smiled as she watched them and, releasing her arms from around her body, she opened them out to her sides so she could capture the energy from around her. With her senses heightened, she was able to catch small jolts of electricity from the people who bumped her as they swerved when trying to avoid her extended arms. Renewed, she resumed walking along the street and became aware of soft pulses rising into her pelvic region as her thighs skimmed gently together. The rhythmic purr, purr, purr of her kitten heels tapping against the pavement enhanced the swaying of her hips and carried her far away from the memory of Nana's washcloths. She allowed her arms to relax by her sides and soon they were swaying effortlessly, just barely caressing the sides of her breasts as she walked. With this newly aroused sensation, she felt alive, alive, alive!

The traffic was heavier as she neared the core of the city. She stood beside a lamp post at the corners of Richmond and Dundas and watched the traffic. She looked through car windows to study the people in them. Married men had loosened their ties and undone their top buttons to demonstrate their rush toward suburbia for home cooked meals. She saw the married women in minivans, complete with car seats and bagged groceries, trying to beat them there. Single men stopped their cars and cursed each red light as a hindrance in their hurry to get home to their lonely apartments where they would find enjoyment in a bottle or on a pornographic website. Stopped right beside them were the single women who blessed the same red light, for it gave them a chance to look at those rushing males. The women would look and hope that their eyes would lock, that they would telepathically agree to stop at the next Tim Horton's for a coffee, a relationship would blossom, and they would finally discover their 'Mr. Right.'

There was a time when Elizabeth had wanted that, too. To find Mr. Right. She wanted to have someone to be her very own, someone to love her and to protect her. She thought of Trevor and Corey. She thought of how each had said he'd love her forever, no matter what, but neither of them could comprehend the black cells. They were both too young to understand.

Continuing to stand precariously close to the edge of the sidewalk, Elizabeth thought of a time when she had been admitted to the hospital and had met a man. He was much older than she and, because he was struggling with his own demons, she thought he might be able to understand the black cells. Once, when they were sitting together in the TV room, he started a conversation about his own difficulties. He told her about the chip 'They' had inserted into his frontal cortex. He explained how They used the chip to control his memory, his speech, his movements, and his social behaviours. He hated when They activated the chip because it made him do things he would never do on his own and he was, therefore, absolutely not responsible for anything that he did do when They controlled his thoughts and actions. Right then, though, They were not using as much control over him so he was able to listen to Elizabeth talk about the black cells. He listened, and took her hand in his. He tried to rub the black cells out of her hand but, even though he scanned her hand thoroughly, he admitted that he wasn't able to see them. She tried to explain where they were, but even with all that rubbing, he still missed them. He had big, thick fingers, too, and when he rubbed her hand, he was too rough, and it made Elizabeth's skin feel raw. She felt a sadness, too, that she had been able to understand his tale about how They manipulated him, but that he had not been able to see, with concrete vision, the reality of her black cells.

A few days later (and after some stolen moments together), he told her that They had finally disabled the chip and that he was now able to leave the hospital. He took her hand in his, patted it less than empathetically, shook his head, tsk'd his tongue at her, and wished her very good luck in learning to cope with her very distressing illness. Elizabeth had quickly withdrawn her hand from his. Really? Really! Mr. Psychopants, with a chip in his head, had the audacity to tsk her and wish her luck with *her* distressing illness? Well, fuck him and fuck *his* distressing illness. Fuck him and every other man out there. She was coping just fine, thank you very much, and she didn't need any man to help her to be OK. In fact, she didn't even need a Mr. Right. She just needed a Mr. Right Now every once in a while.

And today, she thought happily, is certainly a day when I am doing just fine! And, just to prove the point, she ran her hand along her left thumb to feel for any pulsing. She determined that she was free and clear and smugly continued on her way in search of her Mr. Right Now.

She crossed with the light and walked along Dundas Street between the parked and moving cars where the traffic was slower and more condensed. Pre-weekend daters were barely driving, opting instead to scan the curbs for someone, anyone, just up ahead, to pull out of a parking spot into which they could pounce their own vehicle. Once parked, they would disembark for their journey with a partner, a lover, a significant other, a friend, or an acquaintance. Together they'd go to a restaurant to dine while making small talk about the weather, work, or sports. They'd share a bottle of something very expensive and look steadily into each other's eyes. They'd look for that monumental sign that said, "I've shared my meal, I've shared my thoughts, and now I'm ready to share my body with you." They would settle, though, for that small tilt of the head with a slightly cocked eyebrow, a small frown, and the heavy sigh that said, "I'd much rather be with someone else, but I'll go with you."

Elizabeth hopscotched in time to the honking of car horns as she crossed to the south side of Dundas. She

Lorrie Werden

quickened her steps as she neared a restaurant that she knew would satisfy her emerging needs and she passed through the doors. She spotted the "Please Wait to be Seated" sign to her right, ignored it, and quickly veered left toward a small, welcoming table. It was in the corner near the front window, a spot which would allow her to be part of the buzz of the restaurant, but where she could still have her own space.

Elizabeth could remember when this establishment used to be a huge, open restaurant with bright green booths, drooping fluorescent lights, and MacDonald tartan wallpaper. It was a mom and pop operation that served deep-fried goodness to the hungry masses until 2007 when the pop passed away, and the mom retired. There had been a report about it on A-Channel News wherein the newscaster, Kathy Meuller, had called it an end to an historic era that would change the look of downtown. It certainly did. The new owners wanted to provide the area with some updated life, so they divided the footprint of the building; the front became an intimate eatery and the back offered an area of entertainment. To entice diners in, they ripped out the booths, replaced the plaid on the walls with muted tones of grey and cerulean blue, and installed pretty pendant lights so that diners could barely see their food on the industrial-look tables. To keep the diners there, the back room enticed them with both its amply stocked bar and barmaids, a small dance floor, and, for new and upcoming local bands, a raised platform that acted as a stage upon which they could have a chance to perform and hone their skills. When the weekend bands were not playing, a sound system drew people onto the dance floor with a blending of generational music, everything from The Beatles to the latest Coldplay.

The owner's gamble with the extreme makeover paid off when other businesses in the area followed suit with upgrades and refurbishes to their own businesses. And suddenly, that particular section of Dundas Street became the place-to-be for baby boomers and millennials alike. From hemp wear to homeware, comic books to cook books, jelly beans to coffee beans—that section of Dundas Street had it all.

Elizabeth settled at her chosen table so that her back was to the tinted front window and she faced into the restaurant. From this vantage point, she could watch the people as they played out their roles for the evening and wondered who would leave alone, and who, although in the accompaniment of another, would leave still lonely. She would leave with someone. She was sure of that. She'd been lonely long enough and tonight, while her senses were primed and invigorated, she would share her body with someone. In return, she'd receive total ecstasy of body, mind, spirit, and soul. Nana's warnings about the one-eyed devil would not be heeded tonight.

She looked at the women holding their wine glasses seductively against their cheeks and watched as the reflection of the red wine illuminated their lips. She looked at the men sitting across from those women, lust in their eyes as they hungered for a taste of those moist, wine-laden lips. When the waiter came to bring her a menu, he asked her if she would like to start with something from the bar and, as her tongue traced along her bottom lip, she answered, "Red wine, please." She, too, wanted to feel the sexual sensation of the wine as it moistened her lips.

When the waiter returned with the wine, she had not had a chance to look at the menu, but she knew what she wanted. Tonight was the night to show her strength, to be carefree and resilient, so, with this emboldened power-of-self, she ordered a steak very well-done, a baked potato with extra sour cream, an extra dinner roll, and an extra side of salad dressing. She told him twice to make sure her steak was very well-done. "You understand don't you? NO trace of blood."

As she sat sipping her Shiraz, her stomach growled. It had been many weeks, maybe even months, since she had really enjoyed eating a meal. That medicine took her appetite away and, when she was on it, she'd pick and peck at food that tasted to her like plastic and sawdust when she eventually swallowed. She didn't eat much either when she was in the throes of a cycle, which seemed to be a lot recently, but right now her mouth watered in anticipation of being capable of enjoying a good meal. She finished her drink and waved down the waiter for a second.

When her meal finally arrived, she sat over the plate like a pagan god ready to receive a sacrificial virgin. Her knife and fork were poised, ready to be her instruments of destruction. Although Nana usually made her say grace

Black Blood

before she ate, tonight, no god was going to bless this meal. Each bite, each chew, each swallow, was going to be an oblation to her own soul and strength. She jabbed the steak with the fork, cut off a chunk, and began to eat as if she had not eaten for years. Steak, potato, salad, bun, a drink. Steak, potato, salad, bun, a drink. She was conscious of how quickly she was eating, but found it very difficult to slow down. Had she been at home, or even alone at the halfway house, she might have picked up the food with her fingers, gorging herself with every bite. But she knew better than to do that in a public place. She glanced at the people around her. They were not watching her. They were too involved in their own meals and deals to pay her any attention.

Elizabeth smiled and relaxed a little. No one was watching her. She chewed her bite of steak and as she chewed, she could feel the food mix with her saliva and groaned with pleasure as it slid down her throat when she swallowed. She followed that with an oozing bite of sour cream-laden potato, a crisp bite of overdressed salad, a buttery bite of bun, and a cooling swig of her wine.

She was nearing the end of her meal, and as she cut her next-to-last bite of steak, a strange pulse in her left wrist caused her arm to jerk out in front of her, hurling the fork from her hand. She knew instantly what it was. A black cell. She threw the knife down onto the table, grabbed her wrist, and, frozen in place, she waited to feel another pulse. Wait for it, wait for it, wait for it.

Lorrie Werden

With her head bent slightly forward as she tried to feel for another pulse, from the corner of her eye, she caught a glimpse of the remaining steak on her plate. There, in the middle, right up against the bone, was a teeny-tiny trace of bloody red. In an instant she was so repulsed that she pushed herself up and out of her chair and stood with her back against the wall. Her left arm, splayed out on the wall, was extended away from her body and bent at the elbow like a pose from a second-rate English actor portraying Juliette. Waiter, Waiter. Wherefore art thou, Waiter? Had she said that out loud because the waiter was there instantly and asked if something was wrong? She had to think quickly. "No, no, I've just eaten enough, thank you," she assured him, still staring at the steak. Motioning with her head toward the dish, she added, "Can you take that away, please?" She desperately needed to be on her own; she needed to go to the bar so she could search for the black cells. She asked if she could have her bill now, please. An invoice was promptly produced, the meal was whisked away, and the fork retrieved from the floor as the waiter retreated. From the purse that was still over her shoulder, Elizabeth fumbled with her right hand for some money from her wallet and threw it on the table. She spun the purse around to her back, grabbed her drink with the same hand, and ran with her stiff left arm leading her into the bar.

The music seemed very loud in here, though she hadn't noticed the volume while she was eating. She took her drink and moved to a table at the far end of the room, close to

Black Blood

a speaker. She climbed up on the pub chair and grabbed hold of her wrist. There were more black cells now. They made her very nervous. She could feel each one pulse as it passed from her wrist to a collection spot in the palm of her hand, just at the base of her thumb. She tried to rub them out of that area, so they would disappear, but they just kept collecting there. Her thumb was unresponsive under the pressure of the black cells. She continued to rub, and then, as quickly as it came, the pulsing stopped. With eyes closed, she raised her hands slightly above her head and ran the fingers of her right hand back and forth, like a blind woman reading Braille, over that part of her palm. She had to count the black cells. Silently mouthing the numbers as she slowly and methodically traced the outline of each cell, she counted more than 20 of them.

She sat very still in this position for several minutes to make sure the pulsing was done. When she was convinced, she lowered her arms. Although she could feel them in her thumb, the cells were not the rock solid, heavy kind that would render her hand useless. She could still move her fingers and she continued to have feeling in the tip of her thumb, so she knew the black cells would not paralyse her. These were the kind of cells that could, might, go away on their own. She shoved the aggrieving hand under her buttocks so she wouldn't be reminded of the black accumulation and turned in her chair so that her left ear was almost touching the speaker. The pounding of the music would surely block out her thoughts of the black cells and she would be able to carry on with her evening.

A waitress came over and yelled if she would like another drink. Her glass of wine was nearly empty and she was unexpectedly hot and very thirsty. She definitely needed something to drink and her mouth ordered a beer with a whiskey shooter. As soon as she'd ordered it, she wondered what had possessed her to order what she thought of as a man's drink. Elizabeth knew she should have stopped after the glass of wine, and that she really wasn't supposed to drink when she was on that medicine, but she reasoned that now that she wasn't on that medicine, it didn't matter! She quickly called out to the waitress that she wanted a tall glass of water, too, please. With the black cells having arrived, she needed to begin cleansing her blood. Soap and water, Nana had said, would wash away the outside dirt, but only the blood of the Holy Christ could clean her on the inside. She hadn't understood that as a child and she still didn't. The thought of someone else's blood spreading and mixing with her own nauseated her. She must not think about the blood. Tonight she was here for fun and any black cells she had on the inside of her palm would soon be washed away by the water.

As her eyes became more accustomed to the dimmed lighting, she began to focus on the people in the bar and started to classify them. Old man: probably a wino, probably unemployed, probably divorced. Couple: holding hands, but too old to be on a 'date' (God, get a room!). A young couple:

Black Blood

Touching, closing in toward one another, definitely involved. He'll get lucky tonight, thought Elizabeth.

Her indexing was interrupted when the waitress set down the drinks before her and asked for payment. Elizabeth was able to produce the required amount from her wallet with much more ease now, and when the waitress left, she arranged the glasses in front of herself from left to right, the order in which she would drink them. First the water, then the beer, then the whiskey chaser. She swallowed the water in 25 mouthfuls, counting carefully. Then she started on the beer. After she had taken 10 quick nips, she needed a breather. She set the glass back onto the table and continued her search of the room.

At one table, she noted three single males. She wasn't actually sure they were single, but they were in attendance sans women. Two of them, one with brown hair, and the other a ginger, were talking privately. Their heads were bent together and they were smiling and snickering between themselves. The brown-haired man glanced in her direction, chuckled as he looked at her, then, averting his eyes, he spoke to the third man whose back was towards Elizabeth. It appeared the brunette was sharing a joke, but the third man was not impressed. He slowly looked over his shoulder at Elizabeth. He smiled a gentle, understanding smile in her direction, nodded his head somewhat, and then returned his attention to his friends. Elizabeth was surprisingly warmed by the thought of him. (Don't stare! Don't stare!) She saw him rise from his bar stool and watched as he started to come toward her. She quickly absorbed his vision. He was not too tall and he walked with confidence as he crossed the dance floor. He had piercing cyan blue eyes that she noticed as soon as he stood up. He had no facial hair and his blond hair was brushed back from his face and held there by some kind of pomade. He wore black, boot-cut jeans with a brown belt and brown, Brogue shoes. His white button-down shirt was tucked in and he had carefully, and evenly, rolled the long sleeves to just below his elbows. He wore no t-shirt under it, and as he neared, Elizabeth also noted that his chest appeared to be hair free as well. He smiled as he came closer to her table and when he was within shouting distance, given the volume of the music pounding from the speaker at her head, he asked if he might join her. (Oh, God! Oh, God!) She nodded her approval. He raised himself up onto the seat beside her, placed his drink in front of himself and, after they had made their introductions, he kindly inquired about her arm. He wasn't being nosey, he said, but was she alright? "Muscles spasms," she explained, "from an injury when I was working out. It's the only way to get the cramp out of it." She withdrew her hand from her under her bottom and placed it in her lap. She joined her hands together and felt for the black cells. They were still there, but they were quiet. She tried to wiggle her thumb but it moved only at the first knuckle and not at the joint where it attached to her hand, the location of the black cells. The rest of her fingers were free though, and she flexed them opened and closed.

Black Blood

After sitting silently for a few moments, Cyan Man asked if she wanted to dance and she nodded excitedly. She slid from her chair and nervously offered her right hand to him and let him lead her to the dance floor. The music genus being looped through the sound system for the night was favourites from the 70's and 80's. When they reached the dance floor, the final strains of *Maggie Mae* were fading away and an unmistakeable beat replaced them. She recognized the tune immediately—Clarence Carter's *Strokin'*. She closed her eyes and became totally captivated by the rhythm. This was one of her favourite songs, but Nana would never have let her listen to gyrating music like this; it was the devil's music and it was evil. Tonight, though, that didn't matter. Her hips began to throb and she rolled them side to side, in time to the music. *Strokin' to the east. Strokin' to the west.* Elizabeth heard Clarence stroking on a couch and on the back seat of a car. She moved her swaying body closer to Cyan Man and was completely oblivious to the effect it was having on him but from somewhere in the room, cheers and encouragement were being issued from his two friends.

When the song was over, the pace of Elizabeth's dancing slowed as the music changed to something by Lou Rawls. She didn't recognize the song; they all sounded the same to her. She just heard his deep, sexy voice, willing her body nearer to her companion. She wrapped her arms around Cyan Man's neck and held him close, pressing her hips against him. She could feel his body stiffen away from her as she tried to get close to him but she didn't care. She just wanted to be close to someone and to feel enveloped by that someone. After a few moments of his stiffened body continuing to back away from her, Cyan Man proclaimed that he was thirsty and steered her back to their drinks at the table.

Although she hadn't wanted to stop dancing, she was glad to be going back. She was thirsty, too, and she finished off the beer, then threw back the shooter. She raised her hand and called for another round.

"Um," he asked shyly, "have you had a lot to drink?"

"Nope!" she responded. "I'm just getting started." She slammed her raised hand down onto the table and let out a large guffaw but did not notice that this action sent a recoiling jolt through her table mate. "Well," he floundered, as he slid off the pub chair. "It was really nice meeting you, but I have to get back to my friends." He left even before the drinks arrived. Elizabeth was oblivious to his departure. She remained immersed in the music and created her own dance world right there on her stool. Her hips swayed back and forth, grinding against the seat of the stool. The waitress returned with her drinks and Elizabeth paused long enough in her grinding to throw several large bills onto the table. "Keep the change," she chirped. The waitress offered her thanks, scooped up the money, and continued on her way, providing others with their ordered libations.

Elizabeth looked at the drinks, did not bother to put them in any kind of order, but instead reached for what was closest at hand. She threw back the whiskey shooter and reached for the beer, but as her hand extended to reach the glass, she felt it being encased in a larger hand. She hadn't even noticed that the brown-haired man was now standing at her table. He had huge Van Dyke brown eyes that seemed to pierce her soul as she strained her eyes to focus on him. He leaned forward so that his mouth was very near to her ear and asked if she would care to dance. She closed her eyes as she inhaled the Agua Di Gio that permeated from his gold chain encrusted neck. She held still for a moment as the scent entered her nostrils and into her nasal cavity. It lingered there while memories of Corey's touch, his heat, and his passion replaced the scent, filling her with a physical need so strong that she had to rend herself backwards and away from this man. She needed to be able to look him directly in his Van Dyke eyes, not only so she could respond to his question, but also so that he could look, once again, into her soul. "Absolutely," was her whispered response.

She followed him to the dance floor and it didn't matter now what the music was. She just wanted to be close to this man. She plastered herself to him; her derelict left hand was placed around his delicious neck and she wrapped her right arm around his waist, pulling him into her. She opted to nestle her head on his shirt, rather than on his hairy chest, exposed as it was down to the fourth opened button; she did not want to get her hair entangled in the chains when she enshrouded her face with his odour. With the fingers of her right hand, she teased the tail of his shirt out of his belted pants so she could make contact with the skin of his lower back. It was smooth and warm and she ran her fingers lightly back and forth along the top of the waistband. She moved with him, completely lost in his closeness.

Van Dyke instantly picked up on this need for closeness. She oozed the need for sex, to be fucked, and that was exactly what he had in mind. He draped his right arm behind her shoulders and his other hand, much in the same fashion as Elizabeth's, had found its way to the top curve of her ass. By bending slightly at the waist, he was able to reach down far enough that he cupped a good portion of it and pulled her forward to him. She was a petite little thing, but the grip that she had around his neck was so tight, that when he tried to straighten his back, he lifted her right up off the floor. Holding her aloft with his right arm, he moved his left hand farther down so that he was able to cup her entire cheek. With a knock of his hip against her, temporarily separating her from him, he was able to hoist her up higher so that their groins were matched. Her feet rested atop of his and he slid his hand from around her cupped buttocks down her hip, and lifted her left leg up to wrap around his hip.

He was glad there were other people on the dance floor. Everyone seemed to be in their own world of dancing and grinding to the music. It was incredibly loud in the bar, but all he could sense was her closeness and her grinding against him. She used his foot upon which she was standing as leverage, pushing up on her toes to rotate her hips against his. And then she could feel it. As she ground into him, she could feel the bulge begin to swell against her. She was very thankful for the flowing skirt she was wearing; it hid the erection that was being holstered by his pants. When it was rock solid against her, Van Dyke suddenly unleashed her leg and allowed her to slide down so that her feet were back on the floor. He backed his pelvis away from her and allowed his body to turn so that her grinding was once again on his hip. This allowed him time to gain control over himself and they continued to dance that way.

They returned to the table several times for their drinks, but always found their way back to the dance floor. Elizabeth did not speak much during this time, only enough to answer his questions. Was she having a good time? Yes. Did she want another drink? Yes. She had become totally lost in the music, lost in the closeness of him, lost in her sexualization of him, and lost in the alcohol.

At 10:00, when they were swaying to Chaka Khan's sultry voice singing, *Tell Me Something Good*, the lights were dimmed even further and from the centre of the ceiling, a revolving crystal ball began casting colours around the room. As Elizabeth clung to her partner, she could see the change in the lighting through her closed eyelids. The beams of colours frolicked across her face for several dances and they tickled her as they went. They were still gentle on her face until Britney Spears' song, *Womanizer,* began to play. It was not a song she cared for. It was too repetitive in both its lyrics and its beat. When something went wrong with the stereo and the song played a second time, the noise, combined with the repeated swipe of the colours, began to annoy her. She opened her eyes and what she saw horrified her. There, all around the room were floating red and white cells. Behind them, chasing them away, overcoming them, were the black ones. She wrenched herself away from Van Dyke and her hands flew to cover her face. He stared at her for a moment, then swooped closer to her. What is it, baby? You wanna get outta here? He didn't wait for her answer. With his arm around her waist, he led her off the dance floor, grabbed her purse which she had finally relinquished to the back of her chair, slung it over her arm, and directed her towards the exit. He waved an 'I'm-gonna-get-laid' goodbye to his buddies, then steered her, with her eyes still closed, out the back door and toward his car.

Once outside, she opened her eyes and watched as she walked, under his guidance, to the parking lot at the corner. When they neared, she heard the 'beep-beep' of the car's doors being unlocked, and Van Dyke deftly moved her aside as he opened the door for her. She lowered herself into the car seat and once he had closed the door, Elizabeth's heartbeat quickened at the sudden stillness around her. Away from the music and the lights, she was forced to take a body inventory and she realized that the black cells had spread from the base of her thumb and were affixed in the palm of her hand. Now, as she stared at them, they were becoming the thick, dense, immobilizing cells. And there were hundreds of them. They began to saturate her hand and it became heavy with lifelessness, just lying in her lap. She sat in the car afraid to move, afraid the cells would spread from her hand and into her arm. It was because of the change in the lights at the bar. The rotating spots had heated the black cells and made them multiply.

She felt the car jostle as Van Dyke got into the driver's seat and she lashed out her right hand onto the dashboard to brace herself against the movement in fear that the rocking would encourage the spread of the cells. He was speaking to her. Where did she live? She told him, her breath now coming fast and hot. Oh, baby, she heard him say, you're ready for this. I can tell. You've been asking for this all night, haven't you? She couldn't answer. She just stared at him with quickening breath.

Van Dyke turned the music on in the car and it was his turn to sing. He flipped through several Sirius stations until he found the right song. The strains of D'Angelo's *How Does it Feel* filled the Miata along with the squawking of his voice. She wanted the ride to be over. It was not that far to her apartment but they hit every single red light and each time they stopped at every blood-red light, the motion from the braking car spread the black cells farther up into her arm, moving toward her chest. They were beginning to push on her lungs. She tore at her dress with her right hand, trying to get some air. Easy, baby, easy! We're almost there.

They were spreading downward now to the top of her left hip. The pressure on her abdomen caused her to groan in fear. How could she stop them from spreading? If they went down her leg, she wouldn't be able to walk. In a raspy, breathy voice she said to the brown-haired man, "Please! Please get me home."

Lorrie Werden

When they pulled in front of her apartment building, she vaulted from the car. Her legs were still working so, holding her dead arm across her body, she ran to the door. Locked! Her keys. She turned back to return to the car and nearly ran into him as he stood behind her. He had her keys in his hand, mockingly, seductively waving them in front of her. She grabbed them, shambled back to the door and with the weight of her body, heaved them into the lock. She flung the door open and when he tried to come in behind her, the force with which she shoved him back sent him falling backward down the three steps and sprawling onto the sidewalk. She slammed the door closed, heard it lock, and turned her back to his screams of *Bitch* and *Fuck you*.

She limped toward the elevator still able to hear him banging at the door and yelling obscenities at her. She could feel the black cells spreading across her hip and if she didn't get rid of them soon, she would lose all sensation in her body. Once the elevator doors opened, she thrust herself into the box and punched the code in for her floor. Sweat was forming on her forehead and her body felt convulsed with fear just waiting, waiting, waiting, for the elevator to finally stop at her level.

When the doors mercifully opened, she stumbled into the hallway, and approached her apartment with a mixture of trepidation and relief. She began to think about what she needed to do to eradicate the black cells. She finally got into the apartment and stood in the small foyer. Think. Think. Think. What do I need? What do I need to do? Water! She needed water. She moved to the kitchen and turned the cold water tap on. With her right hand she began drenching herself with the cold liquid. She used only cold because she knew that hot water would cultivate more cells. Over and over she scooped water onto her body, rubbing her hand, rubbing her arm, splashing water onto her chest, soaking her side and the floor beneath her. She splashed and rubbed water onto her arms, her stomach, her hip, and her left leg, but the soaking wasn't working. There just wasn't enough water to cover herself. She needed more water but where could she get it? From the shower.

She staggered from the kitchen and tried to mount the stairway to the bathroom. Her left leg wouldn't hold her and she tripped on the steps. A surge of angry pain went through her as her body slammed hard against the steel stairs. Recovering from the intensity with which she had made contact, she used her right arm and leg to pull herself up the stairs. Once at the top, she continued this push and pull method to make her way to the shower stall. Sobbing, she hoisted herself up onto her right knee so that she could reach the shower knob and turned the cold on full blast. She clambered in, clothes and all, to try to wash away the black cells. She opened her mouth and gulped at the cold water. Tearing off her dress, she began expunging herself with soap foaming from the loofah sponge. She rubbed her arm and her leg. She rubbed her now naked breasts and belly. She forced the loofah up and down on her left hip and leg, trying to dissolve the blackness.

But it wasn't working. The cells were spreading across to her right hip and slithering toward her right breast. There were thousands of them, millions of them, and if she didn't do something soon, they would certainly paralyse her entire body.

For a fleeting moment, she thought that this wouldn't have happened if she'd been a good girl and had taken her medications. *Forgive me, Matron, for I have sinned*. But that fleeting moment was overshadowed by the presence of the black cells and by her knowledge that she had to do something to rid herself of them. How could she get rid of the black cells? She reasoned that since they had started to collect in the base of her thumb, then that was from where they needed to be eradicated. Washing didn't help, so there was only one thing left to do.

Sliding from the shower, she dragged herself, soap slippery and soaking wet, back to the stairs. Using her hand as a brace behind her, she slid her buttocks from step to step until she reached the bottom. She forced herself forward onto her right side and did a half-assed army crawl to the kitchen. Pulling herself up to the counter and reaching into the block, the small Japanese knife chirped as it was released from its self-sharpening holder. She positioned her back against the cupboard and without fear or hesitation, she ran the blade of the knife across the base of her thumb where the cells had first started to collect. Red cells oozed from her hand. Damn. She must have missed. She didn't get the right spot. She sliced higher at her wrist. She still didn't get it right. She

Black Blood

sliced again and again and again, looking for the release of the black cells. Where were they? Why wouldn't they come out? She cried and lashed again, and her body slipped and slid in the liquid red that poured out of her body, covering her with their warmth. As the red cells flowed from her body, they took with them her energy. Her cries turned to sniffling sounds, she dropped the knife, and sat quite still as she looked in amazement at the blood cells that had formed around her. And she couldn't believe that they were all red.

–17–

Black Blood

On Friday morning, Marnie Jackson, from the Canadian Mental Health Association, called to introduce herself to Elizabeth. She got the answering machine but left a short message to indicate who she was, that she'd like to speak with Elizabeth, and could Elizabeth return her call at the number she was leaving for her?

On Saturday, it was Matron Evelyn's job to do a one-week check-up with Elizabeth to see how she was doing. She called at 10:40 and she, too, left a message for Elizabeth to call her. She called again at 1:20 and left another message asking Elizabeth to *please* call her. She called for the last time at 2:55 and left yet another message indicating that her shift was now over, that she'd be off on Sunday, but she would call when she got back to work on Monday. In the meantime, *Elizabeth, please call the house and leave a message with any of the staff.*

Lorrie Werden

On Sunday, Yvonne was having a Mimosa with her lover when she started thinking about Elizabeth. She called her and got the answering machine. She left a message about an upcoming exhibit in Toronto to which she was going and that in July she was going to an art auction in New York to purchase, hopefully, a painting for a client, and had Elizabeth started to paint again and when she had, to please call her so they could think about a showing and finally, the call ended with, *Give me a call, Girlie!*

On Monday, Matron Evelyn arrived at 3:00 for her afternoon shift. She checked the phone logs to see if Elizabeth had called back. She asked Matron Annette if she had tried, as she had promised, to contact Elizabeth yesterday. *Oh, I got so busy that I completely forgot! Sorry. Well, you'll have a chance to call her today.* At 3:37 Matron Evelyn called Elizabeth and tried to leave a message, but the answering machine was now full. A worried Matron completed her shift and when she tucked herself into bed, made sure to remember Elizabeth in her night-time prayers.

The following morning, Tuesday, and on her own time, Matron Evelyn went to Elizabeth's apartment and buzzed the building manager after there continued to be no response to her repeated pumps of Elizabeth's buzzer. When he answered, she explained her concern to him and asked to be let into Ms. Devereux's apartment. The building manager rhymed off all sorts of legal reasons why he could not do that, but Matron Evelyn restated her case and asked please, could she at least come into the building? There was a long buzzing sound and Matron Evelyn entered the building. Greeting her in the vestibule, the well-dressed building manager, who occupied one of the main floor apartments, and who was very familiar with Elizabeth, apologized profusely, but he just could not legally let her into the apartment. Matron Evelyn, who had no use for modern technology such as her own mobile phone, then asked the well-dressed building manager if she might use his phone. He consented, and asked Matron Evelyn to please follow him into his apartment, where he handed her the cordless phone so that she could dial 9-1-1.

On the second ring, a female voice came over the phone and said, "Police Services. What is your emergency?" Matron Evelyn explained who she was and indicated to the voice that she needed police assistance in conducting a wellness check on a newly released resident of the St. Rachel's House who, she believed, may well be in a crisis within her apartment. The dispatcher obtained the necessary address information and indicated that a car would be immediately sent over. Matron Evelyn plunked herself down on the well-dressed building manager's chair, folded her hands in her lap, and waited.

Twelve minutes later, Constables Derek Yuoman and Raj Kapoor arrived at the apartment building and buzzed the apartment of the well-dressed building manager. They were let into the foyer where they were met by the well-dressed building manager and Matron Evelyn. She introduced herself to them and reiterated to them her concerns for Elizabeth. Constable Yuoman was familiar with Elizabeth, having been on-site the evening of her dive into the fountain at Victoria Park. He agreed with Matron Evelyn that a wellness check needed to be performed and the four people entered the elevator to ride silently to Elizabeth's floor. They flocked to her apartment with Matron Evelyn bull-headedly leading the way. Constable Kapoor had to squeeze between Matron Evelyn and the door to Elizabeth's apartment so that he could knock. They strained to listen, but there was no answer. Constable Yuoman asked Matron Evelyn to please, step back and away from the door, so that he could join his partner. Constable Kapoor knocked again but this time he called out, "Ms. Devereux?" The constables looked at one another and, as Constable Kapoor stepped away from the door, he asked the well-dressed building manager to please unlock it. The well-dressed building manager, with key readied in his hand, solemnly advanced forward and put the key in the lock. They heard the clunk sound of the locking mechanism being released and the well-dressed building manager backed away from the door as solemnly as he had come. He took his place behind Matron Evelyn and watched.

Constable Kapoor turned the door handle and pushed the door partially open. He could hear water running and looked to his partner with a silent, *Do you hear that, too?* With an almost invisible nod of his head, Constable Yuoman indicated that he, too, could hear the noise. With his hand still on the door knob, the officer called out to Elizabeth, "Miss Devereux, this is Constable Kapoor of the London Police Department. Do you need assistance?" There was no answer, but as he pushed the door open a bit more, he could smell her, and he knew it was too late.

He followed protocol. "Miss Devereux, I am going to open the door now and enter your apartment so that I can assist you. Do you have any objections to that?" He turned to Matron Evelyn and the well-dressed building manager and told them to remain in the hallway. Constable Yuoman turned his head towards his radio, pushed the button, identified himself, and asked for an ambulance to be sent to this apartment address at the end of Wellington Street. He instructed the well-dressed building manager to return to the front door so that when the EMS workers arrived, they could be let into the building and brought up the elevator to this apartment.

Constable Kapoor looked back at Matron Evelyn to ensure she was rooted in the hallway and his look told her she had better stay that way while he and Constable Yuoman entered the apartment.

Once inside, they scanned the large, open room and saw the paint-covered windows and flooring. They saw the opened, spilled, cans of acrylic paint spread from one side of the room to the other. They noted that water was still running from the taps of the sink on the east wall beside the row of windows, but as they looked to their left, they could hear yet another source of running water, that coming from the kitchen. As it was dark in that room, Constable Kapoor, who had entered first, pulled out his flashlight to illuminate their path. He heard Matron Evelyn gasp as she entered through the door behind them, but he did not stop to acknowledge her presence. The other officer extended his arm, though, so that she was halted before she could come any further into the room. The Constables made their way toward the kitchen, one hand poised over their gun, the other hand carrying a flashlight to illuminate the path they know they must now trod. They continued to call out to Elizabeth, telling her they were there to help her, and asking her to respond.

Both officers were seasoned enough to recognize the sickly sweet smell of death and the odour continued to assault them before they actually saw her. Officer Yuoman, who had kept Matron Evelyn at bay, glanced back at her and recognized the sign of the cross as she touched first her forehead, then her chest, then the tip of each shoulder. His arm dropped away from his gun and he motioned for her to join them. The officers heard her whispered prayers as they looked into the kitchen.

Elizabeth had slipped down from the cupboard and was on her side, facing them. She was curled up, as if sleeping, but her eyes were open and looking out into the hallway where they were standing. A small knife, now covered in blood, was on the floor just beside her right hand. Although the skin of her face had shifted slightly towards the floor, her onlookers could see contentment in her eyes as they stared out at the pool of dried blood that surrounded her. It was a look of knowing; it was a look of relief. It was a sign that

Black Blood

Elizabeth had gained confirmation of what she had known all along: the cells are black. All black. Black blood.

And finally, she was rid of them.

Epilogue

I was dead for a week before they had my funeral.

After they removed my body, Yvonne tried to go to my apartment to find something for me to wear for my funeral, but she just couldn't bring herself to get past the front door. Instead, she went to Zack's at Westmount Mall and bought a navy suit. That sounds awful, but it was actually quite cute. The jacket was in the peplum style, and the skirt was cut on the bias so that it flared out at the bottom. I think it's a good choice, and I also think that the skirt would twirl really nicely around my legs when I spin. I also know I will never get the chance to test out that theory, but I approve of her choice. I'm not sure, though, why they even bothered to dress me; it's a closed casket—too many cuts for the people to glare at.

Yvonne arranged everything for my funeral and even contacted all the owners of an 'Elizabeth Devereux' painting to not only tell them of my demise and to invite them to the funeral, but also to tell them that the price of their cherished picture would probably go up in value, and wasn't that a wise investment? That's OK with me.

Lorrie Werden

The service was held at St. Augustus Catholic Church on a Saturday, July 3, the same day Nana was buried.

I was there at my funeral, but I didn't attend the service. I didn't listen to the eulogies or the singing or the pastor; I just looked at the people who came. There were a lot of people there that I recognized. Most were the people who had purchased my paintings, the needy ones who had wanted to touch me. But I also saw that Mrs. Margalis was there and, in hindsight, I realized how much of her own time and effort she had spent in helping me to get that scholarship and, although I didn't complete my degree, I wondered if she was pleased at how well I had done. She was seated beside My Man, the counsellor from Western, and I wished that I had been more attentive back then so that I could now remember, and pronounce, his real name.

A very pregnant Angela was there with her husband and, although I had to look quite intently to try to place her aged face, sitting near the back, next to the stained glass window of the Patron Saint Elizabeth, was the lady who, all those years ago, had made me a peanut butter sandwich and had looked after me when they took my mother away. I wondered how, after all these years, she had remembered me, and as I looked at her, the sun began to shine through that stained glass and once again illuminated my childhood angel.

There was another face among the mourners to which I was drawn, but I could not place how, or why, I recognized her. I tried to recall her from my catalogue of 'known people,' but I could not place her as a former social worker, nor was

Black Blood

she a former teacher. I wondered if she was perhaps a nurse who had cared for me during a hospital stay as I felt protected and safe by her presence. But it was more than that. As I studied her, and gazed into her face, I was overcome with loving thoughts of playful baths, baby bubbles, and, for some unknown reason, the taste of peaches. I wanted to reach out to her, to throw my little arms around her neck so that I could hug her in a shared moment of tranquility, but, as hard as I tried, I could not reconcile why this face meant so much to me. Whoever you are, I thought, and for whatever you have done, I am so thankful.

In the second pew, in the seats reserved for my 'family,' were seated Yvonne, Dr. Anderson, Matron Evelyn, and Matron Bernice.

Yvonne looked beautiful. Her rich dark hair was pulled back in a French bun and she wore a sleeveless, deep aubergine dress with a modest round neckline that was accentuated by a double strand of pearls. She also wore big, black, Holly Golightly sunglasses to hide her tears, but even their girth was not enough to stop the flow of droplets that spilled out from underneath them. The woman sitting beside her, with whom Yvonne was intimately, gratefully, holding hands, offered her a tissue, but it remained unused. The flow of tears remained unhindered in their pilgrimage of grief.

Matrons Evelyn and Bernice were also moved. Matron Bernice sat with her crossed arms atop her rotund belly. With each sniffle and silent cry that required an intake of oxygen, her belly inflated, raising those crossed arms up and down as if she were waving goodbye to me. She had no smile on her face, no smile for me that I had been 'REHABILITATED,' but in my death, her genuine sorrow meant more to me than that figurative smile, and I was immensely grateful for everything she had done for me.

Matron Evelyn, whom I had entrusted to carry my beloved painting paraphernalia back to my apartment, sat silently. She used a tissue to occasionally dab at her eyes to wipe away the tears or to dry off the end of her running nose. She spent the ceremony staring most intently at the picture of me that was resting on my paint easel in front of my casket. I don't know what she was looking at, or looking for, but the intensity with which she stared at my picture, and the love that I felt as she stared at me, warmed me through and through and I felt blessed to have known her.

And then there was my dear Dr. Anderson. My heart swelled when I saw him: my grandpa, my pipe-smoking uncle, my friend, my mentor. He looked very different. He wore a suit and tie—he had dressed up just for me. He sat with his feet on the floor, not folded up and resting on his thighs. His fringe of shoulder-length hair was slicked back and held in place with a discrete elastic band and the resulting ponytail was tucked out of sight behind the collar of his button-down shirt. His hands rested on his lap; they were empty. No notebook, no pen. No recording of notes. No plan of action. I wanted to tell him that I was all better now. I wanted him to know that the black cells were all gone and that I felt free and wonderful for the first time in my life. I moved close to him and kissed him

Black Blood

on the cheek and I know he felt it because at that moment a single, solitary tear rolled down right where I had kissed him, and he smiled.

Book Club Discussion Topics

1. In the Prologue, Julia indicates that Elizabeth doesn't "stand a chance." What would lead Julia to make such a prediction?

2. Elizabeth stops taking her medication. There is a train of thought that people with severe mental illness should be forced to take their medications. How would this train of thought affect a talent like Elizabeth's?

3. In North America, it is estimated that between 20 and 50% of homeless people suffer from a severe mental illness. If you saw Elizabeth standing in her claimed concrete quadrant (Chapter 11) at your local pharmacy, would you assume she was homeless? If you knew that she had a home, would you view her differently? How would you view Elizabeth's mental illness if you were the next door neighbour "who had called the police to tell them that Elizabeth's creative energy (OK, her screaming) was keeping her from getting the precious beauty sleep she needed" (Chapter 5).

4. Nature or nurture? How much of Elizabeth's mental illness might be linked to her childhood experiences versus inheriting the bipolar disorder from her mother? Did Nana's cleaning obsession contribute to Elizabeth's obsession with scrubbing away the black cells from her hands? How did Elizabeth's hatred of being in water begin? Is there a link between this and the cleaning she had to do as a child?

5. After reading *Black Blood*, has your attitude towards mental illness changed?

CPSIA information can be obtained
at www.ICGtesting.com
Printed in the USA
LVHW041446070119
603020LV00001B/37/P